Epic Horizons: Tales of Human Greatness
An Anthology

By Karen Avizur

Karen Avizur

Epic Horizons: Tales of Human Greatness

Karen Avizur

Table of Contents

A Room for One

At Barbara and Ethan's wedding in 1959, Barbara's aunt let it slip that she had just gotten divorced and Ethan's brother was discovered passed out from the open bar in the corner, using the bridal bouquet as a pillow. Despite that excitement, it was the most wonderful day. After that, the couple had their honeymoon at the Cricket Inn in South Devon.

They enjoyed their stay so much that they went on their first anniversary, to enjoy the now familiar Inn and see more of the town. For similar reasons, they went the next year, and the year after that. Now, sixty-five years later, their annual one-week vacation was a staple of the town. Every anniversary they would stay at the Cricket Inn, eat scones, visit the beaches, and catch up on the gossip of the past year.

But this year, Barbara Stevenson called up the B&B, booked a room once more, and made the reservation for just one person.

A car had dropped her off that afternoon and now she meandered slowly down the sidewalk toward her favorite café, her purse in one hand and her cane in the other. Making the reservation for one person had been done with purpose, knowing that the owner would let the other employees know that Ethan had passed. Indeed, she had teared up audibly over the line. That had allowed the information to disseminate properly through the town over the past month, saving Barbara the difficulty of repeating the same words to the many people who would realize she was unaccompanied this year.

Two pedestrians did indeed recognize her as she walked, one on each side of the road, and gave her a small, sad smile as they passed her. Barbara gave her own tight-lipped, small smile in return, not breaking stride. As she arrived at the café, the door was opened and held for her by Erin North, long-time owner and manager, who'd seen her coming through the room's wall-to-wall glass windows.

"Barbara," she said softly. "It's good to see you."

"You too, Erin, you too."

"Can I give you a hug, ma'am?"

Barbara smiled. "Of course, dear." Erin leaned in and Barbara hugged her back tightly before the woman went off to fetch the standard order of favorites.

Her gaze wandering around the café, Barbara wasn't struck with feelings of melancholy or memories. But that was only because those had started as soon as she arrived in town and had yet to stop. It was summer, so even at her age she was able to go out without a jacket, and she found her way to an open table for two by the window. Leaning her cane against the wall, she looked around.

The café had come under new ownership about thirty years ago, but that hadn't changed it too much. Time itself did enough of that. Old photos of customers were still on the walls, but also newer art. And currently there were several large, comfy chairs in the corner, but Barbara knew if she sunk into one of them at her age, it would take help to pull her out of it. She took a long breath of the smells of baked goods and tea and the hint of sea air that seemed to permeate every place in town.

The piano against the far wall wasn't new, but the young woman at the keys certainly was. Barbara gazed at her as her long, slender fingers skillfully danced across the keys, as if they didn't even need the direction of the person to whom they belonged. The pianist simply gazed at the music on the large tablet propped up where, in Barbara's day, there would have been sheet music.

"She's wonderful, isn't she?" asked Erin with a knowing smile, bringing Barbara out of her reverie.

"My goodness, she is. How old is she?"

"Twenty-one. That's Caitlin Williams and it's the luck of the draw we have her," she said, motioning and looking back to the piano. "She attends university and then spends a month or so every summer at a public piano somewhere. Just so happens she submitted a request for ours this year. Caitlin came in, played one song, and we hired her on the spot. Takes a break now and then, but plays from open to close."

"Marvelous," Barbara said, still staring. The music trailed off as the song ended. "That sounded…familiar, but I couldn't place it."

Erin chuckled. "Sweet Child O' Mine by Guns N' Roses."

Barbara gasped. "Of course! Goodness. I've never even imagined someone at the piano with- I can't actually see that far, you won't be surprised to know, but that's sheet music on her tablet there, isn't it?"

"It is. Curious thing. Caitlin's got a touch of magic to her work, so to speak. Actually…"

Erin paused, looking from the piano back to Barbara, and lifted a chair from a neighboring table, setting it down and sitting in it. Barbara spared a glance to the chair opposite hers. She wasn't sure if it was unconscious or purposeful, but it seemed that Ethan's chair would remain available.

Or perhaps it will always be taken?

Pulling out her phone and doing something or other with it, Erin then looked up and met Barbara's gaze. "Is there a song you quite enjoy, that you'd like to hear played on the piano? Anything at all. Maybe…" She paused. "Something he would've liked too."

Barbara's breath caught in her throat, and she nodded. Pausing thoughtfully, she looked at Caitlin as she slowly began a new song. "Young Love by Tab Hunter. Not exactly well-known. These days, at least. You think you can find it?"

"Ah, the internet rarely lets you down," she replied with a wink.

Barbara looked back to the spread on the tray that had been brought out, pouring a cup of tea. Old as she was, she could still pour herself a steady cup of tea, and that was what mattered. Black tea, PG Tips to be specific, was her and Ethan's favorite, and once she'd set the kettle back down, she put in two lumps of sugar.

Prepping a scone next, she said quietly, "Cream first, we're in Devon. He never listened. He always did jam first. Ridiculous."

Erin looked up and smiled fondly, though Barbara was busy preparing her scone and didn't notice. Then the woman nodded once. "Okay. I'll consult with Caitlin."

"Oh. All right then," Barbara said with a grateful smile. "Thank you."

"Of course."

Barbara slowly and contemplatively looped her spoon around and around in the cup, watching the tea swirl. Eventually she brought it to her lips, giving it a brief, instinctive blow to cool it, and took a small sip. Her eyes went back to the piano as the music drifted off, and she saw Erin hand over her phone, saying something and waving a hand at the pianist before walking off to a customer that had flagged her down.

Caitlin took the tablet from the stand and put it on her lap, tapping at it, and Barbara looked out the window. It really was a lovely day. There had been times that, Britain being what it is, they'd had to hustle into the Inn while it was raining upon their arrival. Ethan always refused to be hurried, though. "I don't melt," he'd protest, as he held the umbrella over his wife's head.

Barbara only realized she'd gotten distracted and gone away with her memories when she was brought back, her eyes going to the piano. Her lips parted as the music, a warm blend of romance and a beat that could always get their feet moving, flowed through the room. The notes mingled in chords and notes of the music and the young man's voice, an incredible new, tender version of the song she so loved.

Blinking, she realized tears had started to form and she gently wiped her eyes, then closed them. Letting the low chatter of the café fall away, all she could see was her and Ethan on the hardwood floor of the reception hall. Swaying just an inch side to side, Barbara felt the press of their bodies together and the faint scent of his cologne.

When the music tapered off, Barbara opened her eyes to see the young woman gazing at her, a hint of concern in her eyes, but she was smiling. Getting to her feet and walking over, she sat in the chair Erin had put beside her. "It seems you quite enjoyed your request," Caitlin said softly.

"How did you… Did Erin find the sheet music online?" Barbara asked, clasping her hands.

"It's out there somewhere, I'm sure, but I used my tablet," Caitlin replied. "The program takes a song and transposes it to be able to be played on the piano. Which of course results in a song that's a bit more basic than what a human would come up with, since music is so open to interpretation, but that's where I come in. The best part of playing any song on the piano is getting creative with it, of course."

Barbara stared in wonder. "So, you'd never even heard it before. Your computer made the sheet music in…what, a few minutes? And you just- It was magnificent," she whispered, prompting Caitlin to glance away briefly and her cheeks to warm. "Am I going to see you on a poster in a shop window, for a performance at the Royal Albert Hall?"

Caitlin laughed suddenly. "Oh gosh, no, I've just always adored the piano. But computers, that's my thing. I tell everyone that my mum would get me out of my room and off my computer to play the piano, and when she finally needed some quiet time, she'd send me back to get on my computer again. So, yeah, I wrote a computer program for pianos. Not too surprising, in retrospect."

"My goodness!" Barbara exclaimed. "You created it? How-How does one do that? I know only bits and pieces."

"Well, it's a lot of typing, and thinking, and quite a bit of swearing, if I'm to be honest," Caitlin said, leaning with a mischievous smirk. Barbara chuckled. "It's sort of like writing in a different, tricky language, except more creative. My pa's helping me with the business side, since he's got a few decades of experience more than I do. I'm selling the program to a company that plans on doing it for lots of other instruments. Guitar, flute, anything. They could do bagpipes for all I know."

"You've yet to finish university, Erin told me," Barbara mentioned, motioning in the direction of the manager. "And you already did all this. I feel like I'll see your photo *somewhere* someday."

"That's very kind, thank you," Caitlin told her. "Can I ask…why did you choose that song?"

Barbara paused and swallowed. "I was married to my Ethan for sixty-five years," she murmured. She looked over to the empty chair and Caitlin's eyes followed her gaze. "We come here on our anniversary. Every year. It was enjoyable, then it was tradition, then it was…well, it seemed so natural we couldn't imagine going elsewhere. That song was played for our first dance at our wedding."

"Oh, wow," Caitlin breathed. Barbara nodded and the silence stretched for a moment. "You think you'll keep coming?"

Hesitant, the old woman kept staring at the empty chair. "I wasn't sure if I would this year. But I did. I received permission to spread his ashes, that was a big part of it. I don't know if I'll be here next year, though. I suppose it depends on how this week goes and…how this next year goes. I've no idea how I'll feel at that time. I can guess, though, that as the time approaches, I'll realize it would be strange if I were anywhere else."

Caitlin nodded slowly. "Are there any other songs you've got that I could play? For the two of you."

"Oh, gosh, we'd be here all day," Barbara said, turning back to her with a wistful smile. "You know how many songs a couple ends up with after six decades?"

"Well, not sure if Erin told you, but they actually pay me from open to close," Caitlin reminded her with a playful smile. "So…I'll be here all day anyway…"

Karen Avizur

Check-Up

“I think there's been a mistake. Maybe you're new here. Can you tell the receptionist that you have Heather Martinson in examination? Or you could just ask Mil'kan'it if she's here.”

The insectoid alien who had abducted me stared at me for a long moment. It was funny how a look of stunned confusion was so often similar across species. All it included was a strange lack of movement and their eyes, whatever form they took, examining what was in front of them as if it might change into something more sensible.

“I… What?” they asked. Their chittering translated back to me, as my English had to them.

“The straps aren't necessary,” I told them, giving them finger waves from both immobilized hands. “Everything goes a lot faster if it's easy to move the patient, right? And muscle relaxants and anesthesia mess with results. Plus, Mil'kan'it said some of the stuff they use on humans gets put on backorder constantly.”

The alien glanced at the data on their tablet and then looked back to me. “If you'll…excuse me.” With a final glance, they left the room through the automatic doors.

Leaning back into the headrest with a sigh, I stared at the smooth metal ceiling of the examination room in the alien spacecraft, feeling as if I were at the dentist. The biggest difference being that the lights in here weren't shining directly into my eyes. One of the scientists had laughed when I told him about that issue.

I guess when you've got a certain level of tech, needing sunglasses to have work done on your teeth is comical.

During various abductions, the aliens had actually done a couple scans on me that took a while, leaving me laying down with nothing to do, but unlike the dentist, the folks here were delightfully generous in entertainment options. I'd been able to see two movies so far that hadn't even been released on streaming services yet, projected on the ceiling above me. When I explained it was no problem for me to lay there for two hours if I had something to watch, they'd immediately asked me for my to-watch list. Apparently, there was even one special request from their psychology department for a brain scan to be done specifically while I was watching a movie, and the more complex and emotional it was, the better.

The doors smoothly opened, and I heard a familiar voice say, "Heather! How are you?"

"Ixira," I said in surprise. "I thought you were heading back home?"

The scientist's antennae flicked in what I recognized as irritation as she came over and used her graspers to unlatch the straps on my wrists, ankles, and forehead. "I did. Then I came back, because apparently this place falls apart without me. It's a whole mess, don't worry about it. I'll be off on my vacation for real soon enough."

I sat up, stretching. "All right then. Introduce me?" I asked, motioning to the alien beside her.

"Right. This is Unkiwar. He's been with us for…about seventeen…Earth days? I think that's accurate." She motioned to me. "Unkiwar, this is Heather. She's a regular here. We pick her up regularly, ever since that first abduction when we worked out that she's fine with it."

"Fine?" he echoed. "That's not the typical…reaction."

I chuckled. "This is free healthcare, my alien friend," I said. "Free *hyper advanced alien* healthcare. You know what that means to an American Earthling?"

Ixira gestured her agreement. "Where she lives on her planet, the health issues she struggles with cost an extraordinary amount of currency. So, she's happy to donate time to our research when she also benefits from the arrangement. It was an easy deal for us to make. Being able to pick up the same subject for repeat examinations, with full cooperation? It's been fantastic. Two other humans have the same deal and we're working to increase that number. Heather advised us to go to certain territories on the planet, where healthcare is sparse."

"Yeah, and as soon as you explain the whole colonoscopy thing," I noted with a dry smile, "you get a much less pervy reputation."

"Pervy?" Unkiwar exclaimed. "It's an examination of where your waste exits your body!"

I grimaced and glanced at Ixira. "Just tell him later."

"Yeah," she said dismissively.

"Teeth health is a big deal too," I said, clacking my jaws together twice. "I lost the genetic lottery, and even brushing and flossing like it's a religion only does so much."

Unkiwar turned to Ixira. "I don't understand. Why are the bones in her teeth difficult to maintain?"

"They're not bones," she explained. "Human skeletons are protein collagen and calcium phosphate. Teeth are dentin, enamel, and cementum."

The male alien shifted in a way that indicated an irritated dismissal. "So?"

"So," I sighed, "they need maintenance because they can't heal themselves. Especially since humans live a lot longer than our evolution planned on. If we get an infection under the tooth, it can be agony. And if they get damaged it costs anywhere between my cell phone bill and a new car."

"I…don't know what that means," Unkiwar said slowly, "but the infection doesn't sound pleasant."

Ixira looked down at her tablet to poke and swipe at it. "It's all in this seminar lecture I watched a while ago," she said absently. I assumed she was emailing her colleague, or whatever the alien equivalent of email was. "There. You should watch that one and…this one. Human biology is fascinating, despite the nonsense their evolution has put them through."

"Anyway," I said, drumming a beat briefly on my thighs, startling Unkiwar, "what's on the agenda today?"

"Let's see… Standard examination," Ixira said with a nod, reading something on her tablet. "We'll also need four blood samples, because not only have the labs not gotten their act together about sharing yet, but we have a *fourth* lab that just qualified to assist in research."

Grinning, I chuckled. "Ah, I'm just too popular."

"Indeed. Today is Muscle Day, so we'll be taking those samples as well," she said slowly, "and it's time for another full body scan."

I sat up straight. "Do I get a movie?"

Ixira's body language shifted to haughty delight. "I got you the new Star Wars movie."

My jaw dropped. "That's not even in theaters yet!"

"Apparently stealing a film is not as difficult as stealing a human," the scientist chuckled. "Go figure."

Karen Avizur

Do You Know Jackie?

Well-lit streets, a decent neighborhood, not that late at night. It doesn't seem like the kind of setting for a mugging. And yet? Seems the movies don't get everything right. I'd left the diner after my shift ended, walked two blocks, and as I passed an alley, an arm hooked around mine and dragged me in, throwing me to the ground. I landed with a cry, my carapace hitting the asphalt hard enough to bruise, and stared up at my assailant.

"Your wallet. Now. I want everything in it." I froze, trembling, staring up at the young man my age, holding a knife pointed at me. "Are you stupid? *Now!*"

The shout jolted me into motion, and I fumbled through my jacket pockets for my wallet. Then I froze again, except this time it wasn't from the mugger. A low, rumbling growl came from the other end of the alley. It slid through my muscles like a train passing, priming me to run, trembling in preparation. "Bad," spoke a strange voice behind her. "You are bad. You hurt her. Go away."

The look on the mugger's face made things worse. He almost seemed like he was going to freeze too, but instead he gradually backed away from me like he didn't want to startle a monster into charging, step by step, until he reached the corner. Then he turned and bolted.

Chittering in fear, I couldn't bear to turn around, not even hearing footsteps but knowing the thing was coming closer. "He was mean," the voice said quietly, almost by my side. "I am Charlie. What is your name?"

Slowly turning around, I found myself at a distance that I would describe as 'much too close' to a *dog*.

I'd seen them, being walked by humans. Almost always, they were leashed on harnesses, but the amount of slack and the fact that they were hooked onto the human's belt felt like it was a formality. Once the humans had invented translation collars and trained the dogs to effectively use them, it became a lot clearer that they weren't predatory animals. I'd even met a few.

Then again, there was no denying what it was, that it was taller than me when I was sitting down, and that this dog did not have the cheerful demeanor of the ones I'd seen playing with human children. It was panting, giving me an excellent, clear look at its teeth. Several of them were metal. *Why the void does a dog have metal teeth? They aren't good enough at tearing flesh already. How is it so big? Are other dogs this big? Why is he-*

"Hello," Charlie's collar spoke, taking a couple steps forward and cocking his head. "My name is Charlie. Do you know Jackie?"

"J…Jackie?" I attempted to pronounce, probably butchering it horribly. "Who is that?"

"My friend. I cannot find her." Clearly that was the owner. What was a dog doing out here, alone? Off a leash?

"I, um…I don't…"

"You are scared," he said, his ears going back. Charlie stopped panting and slowly sat down. "I am not mean. I have to find Jackie. Can you help? You can pat my head. It is soft."

I realized that I was no longer trembling, that my instinct to run had dulled, placated by the mundane conversation. "You're not mean."

His ears pricked up. "I am not mean."

Cautiously, I reached over and patted his head. "You're right," I whispered. "You're soft."

"I am soft. Jackie says I am naturally handsome."

Taking a deep breath, I pushed myself to my feet. "Charlie, thank you for chasing that man away. He was…mean."

"You're welcome," he replied, his tail gently wagging. Then it stopped, drooping. "Do you know Jackie? She is a human. She has dark hair and dark skin. Have you seen her?"

"I haven't. Charlie, why are you off your leash? Did it break?"

"I was in the backyard," he answered. "Jackie left. She said she had to talk to a friend and she would bring home food. But time passed and she did not come back. And the sun went away and she was still not back. So, I jumped over the fence to find her. The fence is high, and it was hard, but I had to. I broke the rules," Charlie said, his ears going back flat against his head again. "But she broke the rules first. She always tells me where she's going and when she'll be back. I have to protect her. I have to find her."

Jumped over the fence… Void, how high can this dog jump? "Look," I said softly, "we should go back to your house. If she came home, she'll worry where you went. If she isn't there, we'll…we'll call someone. Okay? Do you know how to get home?"

Charlie looked down the alley and then back the other way before turning back to me. "I can go back the way I came. But what if she needs me? What if someone bad found her, like that man I had to scare?"

Scraping my graspers together, I shook my head. "I'm sure she's fine. Things happen, people get delayed. Why don't you show me the way back home?"

"Okay." He turned and started to walk, quite quickly, and I sped up to keep up with him. We took a surprisingly open route once we'd gotten back to the streets. I suppose if anyone did actually spot him, from their car or through a house window, they would assume Charlie's human was nearby.

Or if they realized he was with me, they'd immediately look away and think, 'That is *not* my problem.'

After about five minutes, we arrived at a small bungalow and Charlie went up to the front door. I rang the doorbell and he sniffed around. "Jackie is not here."

"How do you know?"

"I do not smell her."

I'd heard all about how dogs could smell someone, even track them, so I didn't doubt him. Likely if Jackie was inside, he'd be barking over and over to let her know he'd come back. Taking out my communicator, I glanced at the time and then looked back to Charlie. I felt like I was assisting a deadly toddler. *What am I doing? I've lost my mind.* "I can call the police," I offered. "We can ask if they can find her phone number and call her."

Charlie suddenly darted his eyes to me. "That is on my collar! On my tag!"

Oh, I'm a freaking idiot. "Of course it is," I sighed, leaning forward and kneeling in front of him. He lifted his chin and I found the tags, then stopped, looking at one of them. "Charlie, you were in the human military?"

"Yes," he replied. "I am a strong dog."

Staring in shock, I hesitated before looking back to the tags and finding the one with a phone number. I dialed it and stood back up, waiting as it rang. And rang. And rang. *Come on...*

An automatic voicemail picked up and I let out a long, tired breath. I waited until the beep. "Hello, my name is Tts'ak, I'm here at your house with Charlie. He jumped the fence because he panicked when you didn't come home-"

"I did not panic," Charlie protested.

"So, if you could give me a call back as soon as you get this," I continued, "um…yeah. Okay. Bye." Hanging up, I looked in through the windows, but everything was dark.

"Call her again please."

I met Charlie's gaze, his big brown eyes staring up at me, blinking, and I shook my head as I redialed the number. To my surprise, after two rings, there was the telltale click of someone picking up. But I waited and nobody spoke. "Hello?" I asked tentatively. I glanced at the phone, then brought it back to my ear. "Helloo-oo."

"Is that Jackie?" Charlie asked, his tail starting to slowly go back and forth.

Tensing at sudden low, indecipherable voices, I pressed my grasper against my other ear hole and the phone further against my head, turning up the volume. "…long are you going to keep this up?" It was a human voice, maybe a woman. I wasn't sure I could tell.

"Until…" The only word I could make out, the voice not human. It was an Arkinlatan.

"You can wave around that dinky gun and kick his ass all you want, but Greg isn't going to start bleeding money." My breath caught in my throat. Glancing at the screen of the communicator, I pressed the mute button and then put it back to my ear hole. She was speaking loudly and clearly though, making it easy to hear; it was just the other person there I was having trouble with.

"…be nice…"

"Yeah, would make your job a lot easier. But I've known Greg for a few years now, and as far as I'm aware, Greg will be unable to pay you back if you kill him."

I swore. "No, no, no, come on…"

"What is Jackie saying?" Charlie asked. His gaze and stance were intense, like he could tell I was suddenly worried, but his tail wasn't wagging furiously like I'd seen most dogs do. It was uncertain. Hopeful, but wary, as if it might freeze in the air mid-wag. I didn't answer.

"…kill him…persuade…"

I flinched when I heard a *crack* and someone cry out. My breathing had sped up and my heart was pounding, I realized, as if I were the one in danger.

"I heard that!" Charlie said, his collar volume increasing. "What is happening?"

"Do you know…*Greg*?" I managed to ask him.

Charlie started wagging his tail again, faster this time. "Greg! Yes. Greg is a friend. I have known him for as long as I have known Jackie. Is she with Greg?"

"Yeah, and I think they're in trouble," I whimpered, trying to listen again. But then Charlie was off at a dead sprint.

"Wait!" I cried, running after him. "No, wait! Where are you going?"

"To Greg!" I heard his collar reply. My shoes smacked the ground hard as I ran, echoing down the street. I wasn't exactly a marathon runner, and I was no human, but I worked serving food all day. Being on your feet for so long gets you in pretty good shape. The thing was, I *had* been on my feet all day, and they were unhappy with this sudden turn of events. Sore feet, though, I could deal with. I just couldn't let Charlie get out of my sight.

"Slow down!" I shouted. Charlie had been gaining distance from me, but he slowed a bit. He glanced over his shoulder regularly, making sure that I was still within eyeshot, but kept going at a pace I couldn't have sustained for very long.

It felt like miles but was probably only a few minutes. I don't know what I would've done if we'd needed to go farther. *Yes, I do. I would've keeled over and Charlie would've been on his own*. Considering the course my evening had taken, I wasn't sure if I even wanted to keep up with this dog. We needed to call the police; an assault was taking place. But I wanted to keep the line open, and I didn't even know the address that was our destination.

Finally, Charlie came to a stop in front of a little house, which honestly looked as small as my apartment. The door was open and I realized it had been broken down, the wood around the latch shattered. The dog was sniffing furiously and stopped a few feet from the front porch, on the side of the house that was dark, looking back to me. He pawed at the ground in my direction and, still catching my breath, I walked over to him.

"Jackie is here," he said, his collar speaking in a whisper. *I didn't know those collars could do that. Then again, I didn't know dogs knew what a whisper is. Why whisper when you can talk loud? Or bark?*

"Wait…just a moment…" I wheezed. Taking in large gulps of air to slow my racing heart, I waited until I could speak clearly. "Listen to me. The door is open because it's broken. That means someone smashed it to get in. There are at least two bad people in there, one of them has a gun, and they are hurting Greg. We need to call the police."

"Why did you not tell me they were hurting Greg?" he whispered, his lips curling up to reveal his teeth.

I winced, taking a step back. "I'm sorry."

"Two bad people. Gun. What else did you not tell me?"

"Nothing, that's it. That's what I heard on the phone. Look, we found Jackie. Now we need to call for help."

"I *am* help," Charlie stated. And at that bolted.

"No, wait!" I hissed after him, jumping back to my feet. He stopped short at the threshold, slowly moving forward, and my eyes widened at the abrupt change. I wasn't looking at a nice dog now; I was watching an animal that was hunting. Lifting the phone back to my ear to try to hear what was going on, I closed my eyes and concentrated.

"…made your point," Jackie was saying. "So, how about we empty our wallets? You take the TV, the gaming system, whatever you want."

"…sell stolen-"

Then everything exploded.

My grasper had yanked the phone away from my ear hole before I'd even decided to, barking and snarling bursting from the microphone. Then a single gunshot sounded. Someone shouted, someone cried out, something was smashed. I moved back into the shadow made by the corner of the porch stairs, terrified that the

Arkinlatan inside with the gun would escape outside, would see me, and I'd be next.

My breath came rapidly and my muscles tensed, but in the span of a few seconds, the commotion ended. Waiting, staying still, I listened but couldn't hear anything. Finally, I brought the phone back to my ear hole, then pressed it closer, realizing someone was speaking.

"…call it a night, huh? Call a time out? You made your point, and you'll get your money. Sound like a plan?" There was a long pause, then the human spoke, "Release. Watch." Then there were footsteps, loud and clunky, and two Arkinlatan came stumbling down the steps. I remained frozen, watching them go, one holding an arm, one limping.

"What are you doing here?" Jackie exclaimed.

"You did not come home. You broke the rules! My new friend helped me find you."

"What new friend?"

"She is outside." I flinched, pressing myself into the corner, not convinced the danger had passed. Then quick steps sounded and a human woman came down the steps, looking around. Charlie led her to me, and I saw his tail wagging in a relaxed manner. "See? My new friend! Look, this is Jackie! I found Jackie!"

"Hey," Jackie spoke, her voice gentle. "You okay?"

"I'm-I'm fine," I managed. Glancing at my communicator, I ended the call. "Are you okay? I heard the gun go off."

"It's okay, it just hit the ceiling. We're good now. How did you- What happened? Why is Char here?"

"Char? Is that a nickname?" I asked curiously.

"Yeah, we humans are lazy, we'll shorten names whenever we can," she smirked.

Charlie barked once. "I am Char because I am fire!"

Jackie chuckled and glanced to him. "Yeah, you are." Looking back at me, she nodded toward my communicator.

"You're the one that called? I didn't know if anyone was listening, didn't recognize the number. I was just trying to get you enough info so you'd call the cops."

"Oh… Yes, I heard that," I explained. I gestured to Charlie. "But when I said *Greg* was in trouble, he just ran off."

She sighed. "Of course he did. Alright. Come on in, I gotta check on Greg." She turned and walked off, Charlie quick on her heels, and I gradually made my way after her.

"…right, I can't be mad at you, I broke the rules," Jackie was saying. "But you can't just walk around like you own the place. Someone could have called the police, saying there was a loose dog. Someone probably did!"

"Then what do I do?"

"You…" Jackie let out a sigh as I rounded the corner. "We'll make new rules later."

I swore furiously as I laid eyes on the other human. *Greg, I'm guessing.* "Are you all right?" I cried, catching his attention.

"Just dandy," he muttered. He looked the same age as Jackie and was sitting on his couch, slumped back into the pillows. Blood was dripping from his nose and mouth. I'd never seen a human look like that outside of a movie. A floor lamp had tipped over, two pictures that had been hanging on the wall had fallen, a table was broken, and blood that was two shades of red spackled the floor.

That's when I realized, in the bright light of the room, that the dog's snout was stained with one shade of red. "Charlie?" I whispered. "What did you do?"

"I saved Jackie," he told me, his tail still wagging.

"Those goons will be fine," Jackie assured me.

"Should I call the police?"

"Nah, danger's passed. We handled it."

I'd heard about how casually violent humans could be from other people, but this seemed a bit much. Charlie was well-trained, though. Nobody had died, and the fight was over. It was incredible to believe humans taught dogs not just how to fight, but to survive encounters with violent sapients. "But someone broke in!"

Jackie shook her head, looking at Greg. "And someone learned their lesson." Greg grimaced. "He needed a good ass kicking anyway."

"What?" I asked, baffled.

"I owe them money," Greg told me, his voice grumbly and low. "It's not a big deal."

"I'm not gonna air Greg's dirty laundry," Jackie told me. I had no idea what that meant. I'd learned to just let humans keep talking when they used idioms and figure out whether I needed to decipher them. "But they weren't just thieves, and they weren't just assholes. It's Greg's business. Well, our business."

"It's not," Greg said. "You can leave."

"Don't you be like that," she growled at him, walking over. "Hey." Jackie kicked him in the shin and I startled, as did he, glaring up at her. "You're done. We're fixing this and you're done. I'm not letting it happen again. You are family, you arrogant jackass. Don't insult me by telling me to leave my family to sort things out for themselves."

I looked between the two of them. In the past, humans I'd met that were related had similar skin colors, and Greg's skin was pale and Jackie's was dark. But then again, this was a human I was talking about. She considered Charlie family for sure. For all I knew, she had considered that broken lamp on the floor family.

"You insulting me?" Jackie asked. "Are you?"

"No."

"You insulting Char? Last I checked he has blood on his snout."

"Are you insulting me?" Charlie asked, punctuating it with a bark. I flinched and my eyes widened as I took a step back.

"No, Char, I'm not insulting you," Greg said, suddenly grinning. The sight of a grinning, bloody human made me shiver, but Charlie's tail was still wagging at that same, easy pace. The dog walked over and licked the man's hand a few times. "I'm sorry," he said, the smile dropping from his face.

"Alright." Jackie turned to Charlie. "You're a good dog."

The speed his tail was wagging doubled. "I am a good dog!"

FTL Road Trip

When humanity first set off into the great black void, we had much to learn about space. Primarily, its size. There's only a certain degree to which our minds can grasp it, as Douglas Adams put in his special, succinct, and humorous way. Without the ability to create warp gates and FTL, anything further than our own backyard would have remained an ambitious fantasy forever.

But once we discovered enough of the tech to get to the highways that ran through the galaxy, the far reaches of space were only a short trip away, and we were quite happy to make our own contributions. Curiously we made many, many contributions of one kind in particular. Whether it was our tradition of road trips and all they entail, or the option to regularly mingle with other humans or aliens, or just plain wanting to breathe some different air for a bit, we decided the Milky Way needed rest stops. However, humans being humans, we called them space stops.

An expansive selection of food was mandatory, including three restaurants that, between them, had cuisine flexible enough to cater to all species. Also, half a dozen shelves worth of snacks. Then there were smaller things like hygiene items, larger things like bedding, and many of the more common items found on a spacecraft. The variety of items was limited even though they were plentiful, since the same pillow used by an Ankili would be uncomfortable for a Niltonian.

This was where Ken Fletcher found himself, behind the counter at a register to add up and check out each purchase, on a small space station of no renown. Despite most service jobs being long since delegated to AI, a space stop was largely run by human beings, because of the social interaction aspect. (Except for the jobs of cleaning, especially the toilets, unsurprisingly.) Each employee had their own home, a ship docked in a bay separate from the visitors bay, and they rarely left the space station unless they felt that they'd spent enough years in that one spot and it was time to move on.

Ken was scanning several items for a Zalkinian woman when his communicator, as well as that of every human in the vicinity, let off the egregious noise that humanity had long ago designated for emergency notifications.

"*Cheese* and crackers!" he exclaimed, juggling the cleaning wipes in his hands and almost falling off his stool. The Zalkinian likewise flinched back as Ken took a breath and laughed. "Sorry, those things always give me a heart attack. They somehow manage to consistently hit when I'm most relaxed." He put down the wipes and took his communicator from his pocket, poking at it for a few moments.

"What was that?" the woman asked.

"Humanity's emergency alert system," he said, taking a look at it. "Oh…Amber Alert." Ken took a good look at the photos and description before putting it back in his pocket. A glance to his workstation monitor showed a small exclamation point in his alerts and he dismissed it.

"A what?"

"Abducted child," Ken told her, finishing the job of ringing up the items. "All the space stop employees get them if we're nearby, of course, because we're all over the place. I think we're well on our way to distributing the alert system to a bunch of other species. That's diplomacy though. Not my thing."

The Zalkinian looked distraught as Ken put the items into her bag and she swiped her watch. "I don't think I'd like being startled like that."

"Well, you can turn it off, but it's a lost kid," he told her with a shrug. "And numbers are what this is about. That alert hit billions of screens, but it could be your set of eyes that finds that lost kid."

The woman cocked her head at the rather important point, giving her species equivalent of a nod, and then she walked off.

It was about half an hour later that a large Niltonian stepped aside after checking out to reveal the missing Reptilian child and his father.

Ken blinked and gave them a smile. "Hey there." He tapped at his workstation's screen a few times, bringing up the photos to refresh his memory, but it wasn't needed. Their species only wore clothes on their lower halves, and the young boy had a distinctive purpled pattern on his belly. "Guess what?"

"What?" the father asked.

Ken hit the button for *security* and the other one alerting the closest police to the Amber Alert child being spotted. "You guys are transaction number one thousand for me today," he said with a grin, getting up off his stool. He hoisted his butt onto the counter, spinning around to hop down on the other side. "And that means you get three free candy bars."

"Really?" asked the boy, his nictitating membranes flicking.

"Oh, how nice," the father remarked.

"Now, this is for both of you, but I'm gonna guess you'll let your boy pick them out?" Ken asked with a raise of his eyebrows.

The father gave him a knowing look and gestured. "Go ahead, Hilpari."

Gotcha. Identity confirmed.

"Hilpari, everything you see before you," Ken said with a grand gesture of his arm to the spread of impulse buys below the registers, "is edible for all species." The boy hopped a few times in excitement. "I know you've got your favorite, but that probably means you eat it all the time, right?" Hilpari bobbed his head. "Right. So, I'd recommend just getting one of those. Which will that be?"

The boy looked over the selection before finding the one he wanted, picking up a bag and waving it at Ken.

Ken put a hand over his chest. "M&Ms. Boy after my own heart. All right. Choose carefully. What's candy number two?"

Hilpari's eyes slid up and down the rows of candy, his fingers flicking back and forth in thought, before choosing a Three Musketeers bar.

"You are fond of chocolate, huh?" the cashier asked with a smile.

"Yup."

"All right. Number three. *Maybe* you can get something for your dad, huh? Be generous?"

"Oh, I don't need anything," the man replied dismissively. "He can have all three."

"Hear that?" Ken asked, looking back to Hilpari, who gave another little happy bounce. "Last one, so…" His voice trailed off as two security guards, Rafael and Opal, situated themselves on the other two sides of the father and son. "Hey guys."

Opal gave him a nod. "Sir, can I see some ID?"

The Reptilian suddenly stiffened, recognizing their outfits as security personnel. "Excuse me? I'm just here for a pillow and a blanket," he said, motioning with the items in his hands. "Hilpari, pick the last candy. Hurry up."

"Sir, your spacecraft is currently being disabled until Reptilian authorities have time to arrive," Rafael said, firmly but gently. "You and Hilpari have to stay here."

The boy went over to his father's side. "Daddy?" he asked quietly.

"That's ridiculous, why would-" Ken reached over and flipped the screen of his monitor around, revealing photos of the duo and a description in the Amber Alert. The Reptilian's scales paled, and his vertical pupils dilated. At this point, other customers had started to take notice, stopping as they walked by to stare and listen in.

"Why are our pictures on the computer?" the boy asked.

"Garnilko, please don't make a scene," Ken said softly, prompting the man's gaze to dart to him. "You'll just sit down and eat some candy, and wait, okay?"

The Reptilian tensed and he glared at him. "The whole candy thing was a ruse."

Ken shrugged. "They can take it out of my paycheck."

"You can't just hold us here, it's illegal," Garnilko snapped, making to move toward Rafael. He stopped sharply when the human put his hand on his sidearm. Ken knew the security guard wouldn't use anything higher than level one on the Reptilian, but he'd seen people zapped with that. It wasn't fun.

"No, it's not," Opal told him. "Not with Hilpari in the Amber Alert. We *will not* let you leave with him."

"What are they talking about?" the boy whispered to his father.

The silence stretched as Garnilko's claws curled angrily. "He's my son. I can take him wherever I want."

"I think that whatever's going on, you know that's not true," Ken said softly. Garnilko's glare shot back to Ken and grew more intense. "Hilpari still has one candy left to pick out. Let him choose. Then you and Rafael and Opal can go sit at a table over there and he can eat his M&Ms. I'm sure it won't be too long until they're here."

At that point, there was a fairly decent crowd watching, many humans with their communicators in hand, likely looking at the information in the Amber Alert. And a few of them were recording video, of course. Perhaps it was the pressure of all of them staring, but the aggression slowly leaked out of Garnilko and he glanced at his son. "Go pick out the third candy."

Hilpari shifted from one foot to another. "What's going on?"

"Just…pick one out." The father stared at the floor despondently.

After looking to Ken, who gave him a comforting nod and a small smile, Hilpari scanned the shelf and found his last choice, a Snickers. "Good choice," Ken said with a nod.

The two security guards, with their hands on their sidearms, herded the father and son toward the far side of the room. Finding a table with seats for Reptilians, the two customers sat down and the guards stood by as the boy opened his first choice of candy and started eating. The crowd started to disperse.

"What's going on?" asked a Norgylian, the customer who had been next in Ken's line. He looked at the notice on Ken's computer screen. "Those are photos from the Reptilian police?"

"It's called an Amber Alert," Ken explained, watching as the boy offered some candy to his father, who shook his head in decline. "Some other species already have an equivalent, and we looped them into ours. But surprisingly not all species have one, and not all systems are like ours, so we're working to change that. Whenever a child is abducted, all communicators across the area where the abductor could have fled make a loud alert sound and show photos. Instantly, millions of people know to call the police if they see them."

"Why amber?" he asked. "Does the color have significance?"

"Oh, no," Ken told him, meeting his gaze. "That didn't translate properly. Amber is the name of a girl who was abducted. The system was created after she went missing and named after her."

"Did…Did they find her?" the Norgylian asked quietly.

Ken looked away, back to Hilpari. "Not in time." He watched as the young boy kept eating the M&Ms, his legs absently swinging back and forth under his chair.

I Want to Go Home

If you're curious about how to find a particularly good house to break into on Erilank, in the region of Savarie, it's quite straightforward. It's actually surprisingly easy for a mediocre human burglar like me, and even an average civilian like you may be able to guess. Because even when targeting another species, like the native Norgylians, burgling a house simply comes down to finding a good target that's empty and unsurveilled. In other words, when the owners are on vacation and relying on fallible technology to keep everything they own safe.

The key is not to aim too high or too low. Too high, the targets start to have live-in help, the tech gets harder to crack, and some neighborhoods even have rent-a-cops patrolling. Too low, the payout isn't worth it, but also, most of the valuables are locked in wall safes while they're gone. The key is to find someone who makes enough money that they wouldn't think twice about leaving trinkets in the closet jewelry box that could pay for my life for a month.

The target had been found by Fronic, the Zalk I worked with. I'd known him for about five years now. He had decent hacking skills, and since the well-off folks in this city like to take vacations a few times a year, all he needed was email confirmations. Flights, cars, hotels, even dinner reservations, everything was booked on the Galnet, so we had their entire schedule down to the minute.

That information plus the layout of the house from architectural plans and real estate websites let us plan out the entire job in detail. Then, reading emails between them and family and friends allowed us insight into anyone who might stop by to pick up the mail or a maid service that would make sure they came home to a clean house. Though to cut down on those chances, we always hit them quickly, on the second night they were gone.

The Reptilian with me, Hiralaya, I'd known for two years or so, and I had just worked with her a few months earlier. She was smart but careful, a good combination. The first time we'd met, she'd said break-ins like these were right up her alley. She told me her cousin had gotten overconfident on the jobs he'd worked. On one, he and his people got out clean just under the wire, but instead of that making him more cautious, he took it as proof of his skills and became bolder. He was in jail inside of a month.

After running through the plan one more time, we drove out into the part of the city where acreage was just as important as how many bathrooms you had. Much like Earth, and the colony planets where some people still managed to get too rich for their own good, wasting land was a sign of wealth. Their go-to black hole for water consumption was something between moss and algae.

Our truck was as plain as can be, labeled as an emergency plumbing company (even the rich get clogged pipes, and I can barely picture their type using a plunger) but we still always hacked the garage door to store the truck inside. Once the door closed behind us, I pulled my balaclava down over my face and my two partners did the same with their species-specific coverings. Hiralaya had been driving, and she came around to the back of the truck as we opened the doors.

"Here you go," Fronic muttered, handing over the bags.

We each wordlessly took them, and he left the doors open as we walked up to the house entrance. Norgylians averaged a foot taller than humans, as opposed to most species who were only a few inches shorter or taller, so wandering through their homes was always a bit of a trip. Fronic hooked up his gadgets and did his thing with the security system (I knew the basics, but he was the pro), and we walked in with the door giving a single two-tone beep.

Our process was professional and efficient. We always started with the master bedroom. People keep the things most valuable to them closest to hand, and these folks had a walk-in closet, like most. Any jewelry, watches, tech gadgets that could be resold, even emergency cash, it would be in there. I once found a thousand credits rolled up in the back of a bedside table drawer.

Then, it happened. At the top of the stairs, heading down the hall, a door opened, and someone walked out into the hallway.

We halted immediately and she came to a stumbling stop, a beat passing from shock on both our parts. Muscle memory laid out how the next three minutes would go, an exit plan we always had in case a job went sideways. But that only took a split-second. Promptly after that, I took in everything else.

Standing twenty feet down the hall was another human like me, a girl. She wore pajamas, looked like she had just woken for a glass of water, and was definitely a teenager. The thing was, according to our data, there was no one living there, especially not a human. Fronic was anything but careless, and the facts as we knew them were that there was a childless couple living here, happy to have no one but each other. No pets. Nobody in a guest room. The house was supposed to be empty of anything bigger than an insect.

"Out, go, go, go," Fronic hissed, him and Hiralaya immediately starting to retreat.

I think that the girl didn't panic or scream because her instinct to freeze lasted long enough to combine with our sudden alarm and backpedaling. If we'd rushed her, she likely would've tried to run, but her intuition had told her freezing had made her safe, so she just stared at us with wide eyes. I only took two slow steps backwards, though, before I stopped.

"Hey," Hiralaya whispered. "What's wrong with you?"

It was a good question, but not quite accurate. There wasn't anything wrong with *me*. There was something wrong *here*.

Humans mostly lived on another continent, having settled there a few decades back. Anywhere else on Savarie, you barely saw one, because during the day, the heat waves that were uncomfortable to them were unbearable to us. Maybe some specialized in a money-earning industry and opened shops. Maybe a politician or a diplomat could be spotted on occasion. And maybe the occasional masochist with something to prove. But not this.

I couldn't help myself. "What are you doing here?" My voice was quiet, subdued, and pure confusion.

She swallowed hard, still doing her best statue imitation. After a moment, she spoke. "The…the police… The alarm…" she rasped. "They… Please…"

"We don't hurt people. No one was supposed to be here, and every rule I have says I need to bail out," I said slowly. The girl's eyebrows twitched.

"So?" my Zalk colleague growled impatiently.

"Every rule except one. How old are you? And are you okay?" I asked.

The teenager flicked her eyes from my partners and then back to me. "I-I'm fine," she whispered. "I'm twenty years old."

My eyes narrowed. "Bull." I examined her body and face more closely. My eyes flicked over my surroundings and my memory told me she'd come out of a small guest room. "You're older than sixteen, I'll eat my shoes."

"What are you doing?" Hiralaya asked, her voice tight and quiet.

I ignored her. "Earliest to find work is eighteen," I stated. "Two years since then. The latest you could've started is if you were actually fourteen."

"What are you talking about?" asked Fronic. Something in his tone had shifted and, while I knew both of them would hightail it if I ran in that moment, he knew there was information he didn't have. It was how his mind worked. In our line of 'work', lack of information could get people killed.

"If you need help, you can tell me," I said.

She paused for a moment before I saw something shift in her gaze. A flicker of terror. When she ran, I ran after her.

"Wait!" Hiralaya barked.

I heard their footsteps hurry after me down the carpeted hallway as she darted into her room. She tried to swing the door shut but I went into it shoulder first and she cried out in surprise, stumbling to the floor. Fumbling backwards, she made it to her feet, backing up until she hit the wall as I hurried in after her, stopping a few feet away.

"Are you out of your mind?" Fronic asked loudly. "What are you doing? What's going on?"

"Are you a slave here?" I snapped.

At that, I could practically feel both of them behind me stiffen and stop breathing.

"I-I just work here," she whimpered, stumbling over the words. "I promise, I'm twenty. I started when I was eighteen. I live here. Please don't-don't do anything- You can leave, I won't say anything to the police about what I saw, I'll say I was asleep, I'll say…" Her voice drifted off as she seemed to run out of words.

My gaze was sliding over the room. Not overly fancy, not overly drab. More than adequate. Clean. Looking her over in the light of the room, though, everything about her was the slightest bit off. Like her nails were trimmed too short. And her hair was acceptable in every way except I could tell she hadn't had a haircut in ages.

"What do you see?" Fronic asked, his voice hushed.

Tears came to the girl's eyes and her lower lip started trembling.

"Are you hiding here?" I asked. A twitch of confusion in her facial muscles told me that was wrong. "What's your name?"

A long moment passed before she relented. "Diane."

"Diane. You've worked here for two years." She slowly nodded. "We do our research. There's no one else that looks after the house, is there? You're it. And you live in this room." My palms were sweaty at that point, the grip on the bag in my right hand growing damp. "Diane, why are you so scared?"

Shaking her head, she didn't answer. But the pressure of our presence must have gotten to her because she slowly slid down the wall to the floor, ducking her head. As if trying to disappear.

Taking a knee in front of her, something burning in my heart, I let out a long, silent breath. "Why are you scared?"

"You…you broke in…"

"No. Try again."

Wincing, Diane blinked, and tears finally slid down her cheeks. She wiped them away promptly. "I know what happens if someone wants to *help* me," she whispered, dragging her eyes to mine. "Humans don't live here. The only ones I've ever seen are ones that don't so much as blink when they see me. I'm *fine*. I'm treated well, I'm healthy, they don't even curse at me if they're angry-"

"You don't get paid. They bought you like a fridge. Didn't they?" She looked away. "Diane…listen to me," I said softly. "I'm not demanding you, I'm *begging* you, please, tell me how old you are."

Staring at the carpet, her expression grew tired and she wrapped her arms around her legs. Her lips barely moved when she said, "Fifteen."

"You started here when you were thirteen."

"Yes."

"Where did you grow up?"

"On Earth."

"How did you get here?"

Diane swallowed. "My parents died. I was at an orphanage for a few weeks. Me and all the other girls were selected to go to a new colony on Danu. That's what they said. I was given a data chip with all sorts of information, some family that already had two girls that I'd be living with. But…the ship was intercepted." She blinked back some more tears. "They killed the crew. It was only four of them. And they took us."

Hiralaya swore furiously under her breath.

My reaction was more severe. "The Gibralter," I whispered, horrified. Diane's eyes flicked to mine, narrowing. "The pilot, the captain, the mechanic, and a representative from Earth. All dead. Seventeen girls missing. It dominated the news for weeks. They're still looking for you. The number for the hotline still goes viral on social media every few months."

The girl stared at me warily.

"Listen. I break into people's houses and steal their stuff. I get how that makes me look. But it just makes me a greedy prick. I am not the kind of person who would hurt you. Who would hurt anyone. I am not the monsters that took you, or the ones that bought you, or the ones that pretend you're invisible. And I don't know if I can get you to believe that, but I cannot leave you here to rot. I can't. I won't."

"You have no power," she whispered. "You're not rich or important. If you were, you wouldn't be here in the first place."

"Did you ever consider calling the embassy?" I asked.

She hesitated. "The Earth one? Why would they care?"

"If they knew you were here, they would carve a bloody path through anyone that stood in their way to get to you," I growled. "You and any of the other girls."

Diane stared at me as if I was talking gibberish. "The same two in power who I've seen three times at dinner parties?" she asked.

"No. Not them. The kind that answer embassy help lines. I know humans have our monsters," I said, "but the rest of us destroy them like cancer cells whenever we find them." I paused. "Do you have a communicator?"

"For…emergencies. I've never used it."

"Take it out. Call the embassy. And ask for help."

Diane's eyes held real terror, and I knew why. This was a cushy gig. Humans had no authority over what other species did outside the law, and some of them had real trafficking problems plaguing their planets. The kind that leave scars. Scars you can see, and scars you can't. She was old enough to understand how much worse things could get if the monsters that sold her found out she wasn't willing to stay quiet anymore.

She didn't speak. She just stared. So, I pulled my mask off. Both of my partners hissed in a sharp breath but didn't move. Diane met my gaze more solidly, taking in the expression on my face.

"You call the embassy," I told her softly. "You tell them you've worked as a slave for two years. Tell them you were on the Gibralter. Tell them this address and say you want to go home. And I guarantee you they will be here to take you back to Earth before the sun comes up."

Diane's chest heaved in a smothered sob. "I don't have anybody," she whispered. "If I call them, if you're wrong..."

"I know." I realized my eyes were tearing up too and I blinked quickly. "But you and the other sixteen girls, wherever they are, you all deserve to get what you were promised. A home on that new colony. Choices. A life. You are not spending the rest of your life as a slave. I won't let it happen."

We waited in silence. The seconds ticked by, and I knew Fronic and Hiralaya felt every one of them as a weight on their shoulders. Finally, she spoke up. "The communicator. It's in my bedside table."

I pushed myself to my feet and walked over, finding it and taking it out, turning it on. Doing a search for the number we needed, I found it and went back over to Diane, kneeling in front of her and handing it over. She glanced over it, looking at the URL probably, scrolled down, scrolled back up, took in a deep breath, and selected the number.

A faint voice answered at the other end and Diane startled. It took her a moment to speak. "My-My name is Diane. I…I'm human. I was on the Gibralter. And…I want to go home."

Human trafficking isn't just Taken; it takes many forms. You can go to humantraffickinghotline.org to learn to spot the signs on Earth in 2023, in America, and dial 1-888-373-7888 for help, or look up your country's equivalent.

Karen Avizur

Just Don't Die In My Bar

It was the third day of a six-day week and Haimawa, the Ankili who owned this bar, was glad for it. He kept his bar running at Standard Galactic Time on a seven-hour schedule, which didn't always match up with the day lengths of those coming into port on the space station. But sometimes they matched up a little too well, since a majority kept to SGT for their customers' convenience. That meant weekends could end up with him closing himself in the soundproof walk-in to scream once or twice.

Real dustups were rare, though. Those who hopped from place to place on business knew it was a horrible idea to get on the bad side of their favorite bar's owner, and Haimawa knew many were fond of his bar. It was probably due to him forking out the money for genuine wood paneling that gave it a cozy feel and the bonus of dampening rather than echoing sound like metal did. Also, they enjoyed the fact that any species in existence could find a bowl of something to snack on, on the house, while drinking. Which, of course, helped them to keep drinking.

This evening was easygoing, with two-thirds of the tables full of customers from five species. They chattered, gossiped, and complained, stop-offs like this being one of the best opportunities to mingle with people outside their crew. No matter how much you got along, everyone eventually needed a break from being stuck in a metal box with the same people for ages.

That was the topic of conversation that a Yuluti had drifted to at this point. "My captain was smart when he hired the human on our ship. Did the Santos test. The guy ended up staying for four years."

"Mine just had ours do the Porter and it was fine," a Niltonian said.

"Yeah, it can be fine. But how long is this gig you're on?"

"Three weeks," she replied.

"Exactly. That's manageable. You can get lucky, but it's better to pay for 100 questions to be analyzed on their personality than 10; that's just math. Getting a human match that will stay on crew for cycle after cycle can happen when you use the Porter, but the fact is it's risky, and cheap. And no one likes a captain who you can describe with those words. Am I wrong?" he asked, leaning forward.

The human he'd directed the question to shook his head and he downed a gulp of the beer in his hand. "Nah. I do long term, and I won't even apply to jobs that offer the Porter. You think I'd want to be on a crew of introverts for that long? I'd lose my mind."

The Yuluti sat up a little straighter at the validation. "Exactly. And the happier your crew, the less likely they are to stab each other. Good thing, right?"

The rest of the bar chuckled their agreement in a variety of sounds.

"Food's important too," spoke up the Minakan sitting a few stools down. "Saves money and effort if the human's vegetarian on a crew that's mostly Minakan. Meat's important, but the healthiest of us will eat 80-90% plants. I mean, that excludes me, but I'm here, so that's not surprising." That got a few laughs.

"That's definitely true," the Niltonian said. "The easiest way to keep your crew happy is to keep them fed with good food." There were grunts of agreement. "Honestly, it can be too cold or too hot, the Galnet could be down, and the sewage could be backed up, leaving us pooping in buckets, but if I've got a full belly of my favorite foods, I'm good."

"Here is to *that*," the human said, raising his glass. A few others did the same. "One of my first gigs, we had off-the-shelf MREs. The captain saved money by buying military. If it had been more than a month, people would've spit in his face and quit. I swear, the best flavor in that chunk of gray goo was salt. I would've killed for some chili."

"Oh, come off it with the stuff about humans and spicy food," the Minakan said, leaning her arms on the bar to get a better look at him. "You like flavor. We get it."

"I just said I like chili!" he exclaimed.

"You know what I found out? There's this big famous book series called Dune. You know what the super-scary addictive drug in it is called? *Spice!* And you wrote it *before* your first contact!"

The human's head fell, which left the other customers chuckling at the realization it was true. "That's hilarious," the Yuluti told her. "I'm gonna look that up."

"You should," the human said indignantly. "Those books are fantastic." The Minakan chittered. "What, you're saying that humans aren't the ones that love spicy food the most?"

"No," Haimawa suddenly spoke up, his lizard-like mouth stretched into an amused smile as his customers glanced at him. "Humans don't love spicy stuff. I mean they do, but humans are the only ones who enjoy torturing themselves with spicy stuff and still insist it's fantastic. While their entire face is telling a completely different story. Like they're in a movie, some tough prisoner of war being tortured and just insulting the enemy's mother, continuing to pretend they're not in pain."

The Minakan chittered even louder.

"You can have it both ways!" the human exclaimed. "And no species out there is going to sit next to me and match me pepper for pepper in a competition, you've got to agree to that."

"Oh, no, no, I do not have to agree to that," the Minakan told him. "I've been out to eat with plenty of humans and eaten a bunch of their spicy foods. All the peppers they ask for, I'll always have one. I don't know why you Terrans are so determined to…die on this hill, as you say." The human's eyebrows flickered up slightly at the recognizable idiom. "But eventually you'll figure out you're dead. Hey." She looked to Haimawa. "You have peppers?"

"For any humans who come in here to provide my customers with free entertainment? Of course I do," the Ankili chuckled. The human smirked.

The Minakan took a cash token from inside her belt sack and motioned to the human. "I match you pepper for pepper. Whoever gives up first wins."

"You… Sure! Awesome!"

"How much?"

"Fifty credits?"

She looked to the bartender. "Can you set us up?"

"Sure thing," he replied with a big smile, heading through the door behind the bar.

The Minakan flicked her watch at the token, and it let out a *chirp*, before tossing it to the human. "Don't wimp out early on me just because you can afford to lose the money."

"I appreciate your concern for my well-being," he replied, flicking his own watch at it. "But considering there's a ship I need to be on tonight, as much fun as this is, I do know my limits. And they include not destroying my captain's toilets." He tossed the token back to her.

"What does that mean?" asked a Zalkinian that hadn't yet spoken up.

"It means what is unpleasant going in one end can be explosive coming out the other end, my friend," the Minakan said with a shake of her head. There were some noises from several customers that, no matter the species, were easy to discern as disgust. "Come on. I'm not doing this if you've got some excuse to give up."

"I'm not gonna lose," he retorted. "I'm human. I'm just saying I'm not gonna show off."

"That's crap, you egomaniac," she told him. "If you drop out with excuses, I'm wasting my time."

"Hey, I'll pay to see the show," said the Yuluti. "I'll toss in twenty credits for the entertainment." He looked to the human. "If the pot gets bigger, maybe you won't be such a wuss."

"Teamwork," the Minakan said with a chitter, reaching over to hand it the token. "Awesome."

"Why not? I'll put in thirty," spoke the Zalkinian.

The other patrons started to join in, only a few of them passing it on, likely too broke to cough up anything more than an embarrassing amount. "I'm hearing a lot of donations to the pot," she said after a minute, cocking her head at him. "Are they enough to pay for a sewage bill on your ship?"

The human glanced at the token as it finally made its way back to her and then met her gaze. "All right. Fine. I'll give it my all."

"Just don't die in my bar," Haimawa told him, coming back out from the kitchen holding two small trays.

"I'm not gonna die," the human scoffed.

"You've done this before," the Minakan said, her feathers rising in amusement at the setup on the tray he put in front of her. He didn't reply, just gave the second tray to the human.

"She's right, this is a tray you'd find at Stitchcomb's," he said with a grin, looking to the Ankili. The logo from the restaurant was plainly visible and, while the tray was built to hold sauce, two rows of eight small bowls, they each held peppers instead. From one end to the other, he recognized they were labeled by type, hand-written, order of increased Scoville units. "How did you even get these?"

"I like chicken wings and I've got a friend who owns a Stitchcomb's a few hundred light years from here," the bartender replied. "And this is a stereotype for a reason. Humans come in here and ask for peppers? I don't want to disappoint my customers. So, I keep a few of these in stasis in case someone wants to have fun. By the way, this is my bar, and there will be no cheating. I'll hear a crunch, or it doesn't count."

"You got it," the human said. The Minakan bobbed her head once.

Haimawa nodded at her. "I'll hold onto the token?"

"Yeah, thanks." She handed it over.

He took it and then made a gesture with his other clawed hand. "So, human. Go for it. *Have fun.*"

All the other customers made noises of encouragement and Haimawa leaned over to the stereo controls, turning up the music a little as the onlookers eagerly watched.

Both started with the first row, eating two peppers at a time. "I actually haven't had habaneros for a while," the human spoke with a smile, glancing to his competitor. "I should buy them more often."

The Minakan just cocked her head and then picked up the next two. Haimawa came out from the kitchen, though no one had noticed him leave and no one paid attention to him coming back, with two cups of milk. He set them next to the register and leaned back against the wall, grinning as he looked across the bar at everyone watching the show, some muttering back and forth.

They moved on to the third row. Some teasing, insults. Then the fourth. Some mocking of each other's cultures. By the fifth, they'd slowed down to one at a time, the Minakan's eyes had turned red from the veins expanding and the human was ignoring tears. The insults were getting more creative. The sixth row, they reduced to eating half at a time. Once they finished the second, the two of them were coughing and breathing hard.

"Come on, you can do it!" called someone behind the Minakan. "Show the meat bag humans have died on that hill!"

"Oh, shut up, you giant gummy worm," the human said. He took a breath and wiped his nose on his sleeve before taking a bite of the first pepper in the seventh row. The Minakan did the same. He coughed again, taking a deep breath and letting it out. "This is the best time I've had since I drank a Nati under the table."

"Like I said," Haimawa spoke up. "It's not love. It's masochism. Look at you."

"Just because I'm miserable doesn't mean I'm also not having the time of my life!" he exclaimed, leaning back in his chair as he was wracked with coughs. All the customers were now chatting and laughing among each other, gesturing to the two competitors, probably guessing who would go home with the money.

The Minakan had a meter or so of open space around her now because she kept needing to flap her wings slowly back and forth. "Nati will keel over if you give them two fingers of vodka," she rasped.

"I didn't say it was fair, I said it was fun," he cackled.

Another bite. And then the first of the second pepper. The Minakan took another break, breathing deeply and slowly and flapping her wings. The human took a few more deep breaths as well. He clenched the edge of the bar in his sweaty hands. "Cheeeese and rice," he whispered, continuing to blink back tears.

"If anyone here doesn't know," Haimawa said cheerfully, holding up two glasses of milk, "milk is the best thing for someone who has eaten something spicy."

"Shut up, you jerkward," the human growled, leading to laughter through the bar.

"Fun fact: If you can't find a nice…cold…refreshing glass of milk, a mouthful of sugar has the same effect."

"You're a prick, Haimawa," chuckled one of the regulars from the back.

"Never claimed to be anything else," he replied.

With a flick of her clawed fingers, the Minakan tossed the second bite into her mouth, crunched, and swallowed it immediately. The human stared at her before finally closing his eyes and eating his as well. The Minakan stayed silent, but all of the feathers on her body were flared at this point, some of them moving gradually as she breathed.

The human whispered a series of swears under his breath. "You done?"

The human looked up to his opponent as she took a deep breath and took the first bite of a pepper from the last row, putting her in the lead. Her face twitched as she barely stopped herself from grimacing, but didn't say anything.

Wiping tears and snot across his sleeve again, he took a bite, chewed and swallowed. Then he proceeded to make a series of noises that, likely, no one in the bar had ever heard a human make before. "That's…so tasty," he managed.

The bar exploded in laughter.

A minute passed by, and Haimawa knew both had been tempted earlier to get each pepper over and done with, but that strategy had fallen by the wayside. Instinct had kicked in, and continuing now was a matter of using a whole other part of the brain. The part that, despite evolution's best efforts, had managed to stick around.

The Minakan lowered her wings and took the next bite. She finally let out a squawk of unhappiness, which led to more laughter from the onlookers, but she was in the lead once more. The human was holding tightly to the bar again, as if he might fall off his stool. Haimawa lowered his head curiously. *Who knows? Maybe he will.*

Haimawa watched as the human's right hand let go of the bar, then lay down flat on its cool wood surface. He took a breath. Then another. Then he picked up the pepper…and he put it down, pushing the tray away. "Milk."

"Sorry, what was that?" Haimawa asked the tomato-faced human.

"Give me the milk you jackass!" he coughed.

The bar erupted as Haimawa brought over the glass and the human chugged it. He gave the other to the Minakan, who gratefully took it and drank from the side that conformed to her beak. The human eventually lowered the empty glass and stared at the Minakan, who met his gaze, her feathers flared happily. "I hate you so much," he whispered. It was too noisy by then for her to hear him, but the sentiment came across and she winked at him.

Haimawa handed over the token to her and she left the bar, unsteady with red eyes, as if she'd had one drink too many. The only giveaway that there was something else going on was that her feathers were still prickled high, leaving her looking like a pincushion. The human remained slumped back in his chair, glaring at the tray as if it had personally insulted him, as the customers wandered back to their tables.

"Refill?" the human finally asked, raising the empty glass of milk.

* * *

"You made out pretty good," said Bowwil, staring at the token and looking at Ricka with an approving flitter of his antennae. "Nice haul."

Ricka was laying across the metal floor of the common room, her wings splayed wide, the other members of the crew sitting in chairs or on the couch. "Yeah, the bar was full enough and it was a show." She slowly sat up, blinking a few times. "Still worked the second time around. How long until word starts to spread?"

"In general, humans are gonna be the first to realize it's a hustle," Harry told her. "It's not common knowledge, but enough of us know that Earth birds don't taste spiciness. Once someone makes the connection, they'll just need to hop on the Galnet to check on Minakans."

"You think so? Just a Galnet search?" asked Wiltu. "Spiciness is negligible for Minakans, but they know it still affects them at high enough levels. But no studies have been done, there's no real gossip. I'd think one of their own would be the first to hear something and be suspicious."

"Humans are different," Harry said, shaking his head. "We get real physical reactions. You get high enough on the Scoville scale, you get stuff that's genuinely toxic. Minakans would survive higher ratings than humans could, even after desensitizing ourselves over time."

The sound of the ship door opening drew their attention and footsteps echoed down the hall. "The defeated party has arrived!" Ricka exclaimed.

"Ha ha ha," said Kumar with a tired smirk.

"How you holding up, bud?" asked Harry. "Ricka said you put on a good show."

"Easy money," he grunted, lowering himself onto the couch.

Harry chuckled. "Easy, huh? You're home now, idjit. We're the ones that're gonna hear you swearing when your ass hits that pot."

Kumar groaned. "Fair. Same as last time. Gastrointestinal inferno incoming. But the bread, ice cream, and antacids will take the edge off. Dinner of champions, huh?"

"Champions? You lost," Harry smirked.

"Hey. The bartender knew."

Kumar glanced to Ricka and narrowed his eyes, and the other crew members reacted similarly. "What? You sure?" Kumar asked.

"Uh huh." She flared her crest feathers and chuckled. "There was one point where he gave me a smile and this…look."

"Did he think you were hustling Kumar or did he realize you two were in it together?"

"Couldn't tell. Whichever it was, he didn't care. He knew what was coming and it was going to be pure entertainment," she chittered.

"Oh, the bartenders," Wiltu suddenly said, leaning forward. "We were guessing who'd spot the hustle first? We were thinking about it from the wrong angle. It's going to be the one who needs to know how to feed their customers without killing them."

Murmurs and grunts of understanding echoed through them.

"We have officially proved humans wrong, though," Ricka told Kumar. "You're not the species that can handle the most spice."

"What? Survival is never what this has been about," Kumar scoffed at her. "Minakans can handle more, but humans are still the Scoville champions."

"In what universe does that make sense?" Ricka asked, baffled.

"Because you put up with it; we enjoy it," Kumar told her. He leaned back further into the cushion and let out a breath. "The bartender was right *and* wrong. We do torture ourselves with some of those peppers, but we're deranged." He grinned at her. "*We still like it.*"

Memory Loss

I'd always hated clichés in movies.

"It's quiet... Too quiet..."

Yet that's the first thing that came to mind when I woke up. There were always two days in my neighborhood that made my morning walk with Mikey incredibly peaceful: Christmas morning, and the morning of New Year's Day. It was an interesting contradiction in sources, because the first was in celebration, the majority gathering in their living rooms opening presents, and the second was being miserable, from hangovers.

My alarm hadn't woken me and its red digits declared that it was 10:24 a.m., which worried me, because it was Wednesday. But if I were late for work, why hadn't my cell phone woken me, the shouting of my supervisor jolting me into consciousness and frantic apologies? My ears continued to strain for any noises from the busy city I lived in, the sounds usually recognizable and close, even from three floors up. I blinked away the last remnants of sleep and sat up in bed. And my eyes slowly widened.

Even in the dim light of the sun creeping around my curtains, I could see clear enough to look over the writings scrawled across the wall opposite my bed. The words were written in thick Sharpie on a whiteboard, direct and to the point, in what was clearly my handwriting.

"It's been 712 days. You must figure out how to block the wipe. Follow your notes. And maybe one day we'll wake up remembering. Play the recording on the bedside table."

Swallowing hard and feeling like I'd been dropped into a horror movie, I looked behind my alarm clock to a recorder. My first urge was to quickly run from my room, out the door, and find someone, anyone, to talk to. But something about the striking silence outside evoked a fear response that nudged me to follow the directions. Tentatively, as if it would bite, I picked up the recorder. It had about an hour's worth of audio on it, according to the display.

I pressed play. A shiver went down my spine as I heard my own voice.

Hey, girl, first off, if it's any comfort, you're not going crazy. Though continue every day to, quite literally, lose your mind. After every sleep cycle, your mind resets, wipes itself. You remember the disease that was spreading so fast through every country it touched? You lost the few days when the crap hit the fan and everything shot up exponentially. Hit the stop button now.

Automatically obeying the instructions and putting the recorder back down, I narrowed my eyes as the information started to come flooding back. The perpetrator was a prion, quick, horrific, and relentless. I'd continued my work at the lab as long as I could, following all safety procedures, despite the dread that inevitably I'd succumb to the same fate as all the others.

My eyes darted to my phone and I picked it up. 712 days, the writing said. The clock was still accurate. But the date…

I unlocked the phone and went to my calendar. Almost two years had passed.

Then I realized why the instructions had been to stop the playback of the recording, because my hands started shaking and I dropped the phone to my bed. Closing my eyes, I carefully regulated my breathing. I was alive, and that's what mattered. I was surviving, somehow, day by day, week by week, month by month. Two years was significant, it meant I'd developed a routine, had continued to live my life, despite…

My eyes opened and a thin layer of tears formed on the edge of my eyelids. Was everyone else gone? How many other people were out there surviving like I was?

I slowly picked up the recorder and pressed play again.

Good news is, yeah, you're managing okay. Bad news is, the rest of the world went downhill fast. Suicides, mostly. Mom and Dad are dead, I'm sorry.

My hand flew to my mouth and my lower lip trembled. I blinked, sending tears cascading down my cheeks.

But you're not. *And there are others who are surviving too, just taking things one day at a time, recording their memories like you are. Danny and Kalie in 429 do food; they set up box gardens on building rooftops. Go give them a hug and introduce yourself when you're done here. Aside from that, supplies are plentiful, since the city was set up for so many more lives than it currently supports. We're doing okay.* You're *doing okay.*

But here's the hitch. You've been working on this thing ever since your first wipe. Progress has been made, you know how it goes, but this thing is a monster, especially with the disability you're being crushed under. We haven't figured it out yet, much less found a treatment. So, every day, you wake up and listen to this recording and keep going. Let me say that again: you don't start over. You keep going. The CliffsNotes will come next on the recording, and once you've got the basic info you need, you can head back to the lab and keep working. You moved everything to that lab on 23ʳᵈ, since that commute was just stupid without public transport.

I heard myself take a long breath.

This is hard. But you've got a bit of a gift here. You don't know how hard it's been. The days and weeks and months haven't piled on top of your shoulders. So, start this day like you're cheating, like someone else has been doing all this work for you, and that you just need to keep moving forward. You're standing on the shoulders of giants here, months and months of work from tireless giants. You can do it. Press stop again now.

Obeying the instructions, I swallowed hard. For all the terror and confusion I felt, considering how much I'd lost in what felt like the blink of an eye, and feeling like I'd found myself in the middle of a thick, unending forest with no way home, she was right. I was right. One day at a time.

Putting aside the rest of the recording for the time being, I got up and got dressed, brushing my teeth with water in a bottle next to my useless faucet. I took my dog Mikey out for a pee, the eerie silence of the streets echoing intimidatingly, and I was quick to go back inside. It seems this was my typical habit at this point, since Mikey didn't skip a beat following me back in, delaying our real walk for later.

Then I left Mikey back in my apartment before I walked up to the fourth floor and knocked on the door, worrying at my lower lip. The door opened, revealing a young man and woman about my age, who looked exactly like I felt. Unsteady, worried, but a shadow of determination behind their eyes.

"Hi. I'm Jasmine." I put out my hand. "It's nice to meet you."

Metal Armor

When you first sign up for the procedure, you're given a presentation, and it's clear the presenter has given it many times before, to the point that they wish someone would just make a video for us to watch. The transfer from human to android body is easy and straightforward, as they explain it. But hell if I know how they do it. I know how to drive a car, but I'm not a mechanic.

The idea was the brainchild of one Carissa Blaine, who was somewhere between a neurologist and a mechanical engineer, who made the leap that so many others had been straining for over the years. She was building on the knowledge and mistakes and science of those who'd come before her, of course, but still, her name is a household one for a reason. And I'm sure her funding shot through the roof when they realized it would work.

When they realized existing as a being of metal and plastic would let you walk right by a zombie.

For a couple years now, after the disease that left us scrambling metaphorically and literally, we'd managed to survive in decent numbers, just perpetually on the run, always with a gun in our hands. We lived in bunkers and skyscrapers and when any adult and sometimes the odd teenager would be seen exiting the safety of a barricade, it would always be with a weapon in their hand to help cull the herd as best we could.

Everything changed because of Carissa Blaine, and that's why I was here. Ryan and I had been military before it hit, him Army and me Marines, and we were called to the front lines once again when this unprecedented war hit our planet. There was still no cure or vaccine, and the scientists were conceding by this point that they didn't know if they'd ever figure out how to create one. So, androids it was.

Then Ryan was gone and, yeah, I'd spiraled a bit, I'm not ashamed to admit. Looked for answers at the bottom of a bottle for a few weeks, barely got out of bed. It had just been bad luck out there in the field with our guns in our hands and as much ammunition as we could carry. That's the worst, when you don't even have anyone or anything to blame but fate, when you've got no one to punch or scream at or punish for incompetence. You're just left with emptiness and the hot burn of survivor's guilt.

After the presentation, I and all the others proceeded to what seemed very much like a doctor's office to me, complete with a lobby, receptionist, and magazines to leaf through. My name was called eventually and when I first saw the creation, my doppelganger, it was surreal beyond belief. It lay there in a horizontal chair like I'd expect to see at the dentist's office, with another empty chair next to it, in which I lay down.

There was a lot of explaining of things I already knew, the piles of paperwork already done with, and then I was hooked up, transferred, and woke up with the similarly surreal experience of looking through my new eyes at my corpse.

We were only the first of many. Civilians signed up one after another to become immune to zombie attack (and effectively immortal), though many recoiled at the idea of becoming an android. There was no undo button on it, of course. Even when we won the war, even after a hundred years, if our innards were properly maintained and we lasted that long, we'd still go on as beings of plastic and metal, no matter how much we looked like a human being. Though I highly expected for the military to make use of me in the field in such a case, so I was in for far more than a boring life if we vanquished the last of the undead.

That first day, I put on my gear as I always did, the only difference being that I skipped the protective layers this time. Armed and ready to go, I headed out into the world with a cloak of invisibility around my shoulders. Though I'll admit, that took a while for my instincts to catch up with. My feet itched to run from a horde I came upon and an icy finger trailed down my spine the first time I brushed up against one. But it leaned toward me on instinct and then just…moved on.

Wandering the streets, it was utterly weird, dreamlike, though I'd never had a dream like this. Any nightmares that plagued me always consisted of me or someone I cared for being on the wrong end of a pair of teeth and a jugular being torn out. This was peaceful in a strange way, as if I were just going for a walk among some exceedingly monstrous company.

Making my way into a park, overgrown and choked with weeds, that's where I found him.

No bite mark, it had been stray spittle that had gotten Ryan. He looked just like any of the others, all pallid skin and drooping, gray eyes, in a calm state since he was undisturbed with the lack of prey nearby. The only difference was his thin Kevlar armor, useless as it had ended up being. I blinked back the tears threatening to fall and took the syringe from my pocket. The deadly (or would it be undeadly?) cocktail was usually in a dart to be shot from a gun, of course, but I'd requested just a single syringe.

Walking up to him, I situated myself in his line of sight, so I was able to meet his vacant gaze. Reaching out, I put my hand on my shoulder. That roused him a bit, his eyes searching for any prey, or to determine if he'd just been brushed against by another of his kind.

"I'm sorry," I muttered. Staring at him, I admitted, "I thought about just coming back out here to join you. But I knew that wasn't what you'd want. I knew what you'd want. I just wanted to be the one to do it for you."

With that, I pulled the top off of the syringe. Then I injected the contents into Ryan's neck, prompting another flinch and curious exploration with his eyes and nose, and recapped the syringe. Then I tossed it aside, some part of me recognizing the oddity of not caring about the world I was in, that I was disposing of a used syringe in a children's playground. But not as if we could reuse it back at the bunker, and I doubted anyone else wanted this kind of up close and personal kill with a zombie.

He stumbled then, and I caught him, the burn of tears sharp behind my nose as his weight grew heavier in my arms and I slowly lowered him to the ground. There was no violent twitching, no struggle to survive. He just drifted away. I knelt there beside him, blessing Carissa Blaine for coming up with a way for me to say goodbye. And at the same time cursing her name that she hadn't been smart enough, fast enough, to achieve her landmark invention just a few months earlier.

I knelt there for a while, staring at Ryan, knowing he would start to decay now, and this was the last time I'd see his face, as horrid a sight as it was. Then eventually I pushed myself to my feet, took a breath, and drew the gun holstered at my side to continue my work in the hopes of one day finishing it.

New Neighbors

As I finished chopping the honti and pushed them off the cutting board and into the bowl, I sighed. "We just- We have enough species! Why do we need another? Seventeen isn't enough?"

My daughter laughed at me, her voice echoing through the kitchen through the speakerphone. "You sound xenophobic, you know that, right?"

"I am not xenophobic," I snapped. "I'm not saying they're going to steal our jobs and bring crime with them. I'm just old and I hate change. Just you wait, it'll happen to you someday too."

"Yeah, but until then, apparently I was assigned the job of keeping my mother from becoming a cliché," Likana spoke. "Hopefully Niti won't have to do the same for me when I'm your age. What sounds so bad about humans?"

Continuing to chop the next vegetables for my salad, my feathers flared. "Nothing sounds bad. That's the point; you never know what you're getting. The I'qa came here and I couldn't find any milk on the shelves for *three months* unless I stood in line before they opened in the morning. Not one person in charge of immigration went, 'Oh, they drink it like water? Maybe we should prepare for that!' They weren't allergic to even one kind. Everything. Gone."

"You're afraid the humans are going to drink as much milk as I'qa do?" she asked, chuckling.

"Who knows? When I got a Glamen coworker and the company reworked the 'ideal' temperature, our office was like a freezer until they got him his own room. And when your sister had an Ummian moved in next door-"

"Their ears are different, and you know that."

"Apparently no one else did before they got here! Anyone who listens to what they call music, it feels like their ears are bleeding," I told her.

"Hey, it's all a matter of perspective. Anyone who manufactures sound-proofing materials was ecstatic."

I laughed despite myself. "Yes, I'm sure. Another Frangla incident is all I'm worried about."

"Mom, no," Likana said firmly. "A species like that was…practically an experiment. And the politicians were so pushy about being willing to welcome anyone that they didn't conceive of the possibility that *they* would hate all of *us*."

"That was a nightmare," I griped. "Them telling *us* to go back to Ritan? And their children were little monsters. If it had been Niti's beak that had been fractured instead of-"

"Aren't you making a salad?"

I stopped chopping and looked at the speaker. "Yes?"

"You get angry enough, you're going to mince those vegetables into soup."

Lowering the knife to the cutting board, I glared. "Very funny."

"Mom, I've got to go. Niti needs help with homework. Everything will sort itself out. And if the stores start to get low on milk, I'll buy a cartful and put them in our freezer."

"You're hilarious. Goodbye."

"Love you, Mom."

"Love you too."

Pulling the hose a few feet further to give myself more slack, I slowly watered around the gnola tree in my front yard.

Both my front and back yard were covered in things that sprouted fruits and vegetables. I'd been growing them since I was younger than my youngest grandchild, passionate even for a Minakan, who were known for gardening, and at this point I could probably write a book.

Likana would laugh her beak off. Me, writing a book. That would mean staying seated for long stretches. She'd probably put up a camera to record how long I lasted.

I heard the front door shut from the house beside mine and looked up, letting go of the handle on the hose to stop it flowing. An adult human and a young human, their offspring. I'd read an article that said even experts of other sapient species could be confused trying to guess human gender by appearance and it was best to ask for pronouns. *Long head fur is female, short head fur is male. Mostly. What did that article mean,* mostly*? What kind of help is that?*

The young human caught sight of me and took in a gasp of air, jumping up and down, pointing at me. "Mommy! She's Minakan! We have a Minakan neighbor!" *Female. Ha, I was right, and that's one down.*

"You are *pointing* at her," the mother said in a lower voice, putting her hands on her hips.

The youngster immediately lowered her limb and stiffened. "Sorry."

"Do you want to go introduce yourself?"

"…Yes please."

They must be pretty loud if I can hear them over here.

Minakan ears were quite keen, our avian ancestry giving us the skills to hunt during the winter, but I hadn't even been trying to focus on them. Of course that meant my ears were excellent modulators of loud sounds too. It wouldn't be to listening closely for a rodent in the brush and then have someone pass by and deafen you with a single *squawk.*

"Hi, I'm Marilyn," the mother spoke, waving her grasper as she approached. "This is my daughter, Georgia."

Two females, one with short hair. So much for that idea. "I'm Ackla," I replied. "It's nice to meet you. You're the first humans I've met."

"Really?" Georgia asked. She was bouncing on her feet like she was getting ready to jump and fly off.

"Yup."

"That's a cool name. Ackla. You're the first Minakan we've met too! You're *so* pretty!"

I blinked rapidly, my head pulling back a bit. "Thank-Thank you."

"Do you know much about Earth?" Marilyn interjected.

"Ah, no, sorry."

"To give you some context for Georgia's excitement, there are an incredible amount of avian species called *birds* on our home planet. And they are her favorite animal."

Georgia immediately looked up to her mother. "*No.* My favorite animals aren't just birds," she said. My crest feathers lifted just slightly in surprise and amusement at the reprimand in the child's voice. "You can't just say birds; there are ten thousand kinds of birds on Earth. My favorites are crows. You *know* that."

"Absolutely, my mistake," Marilyn said, her mouth wide to show her teeth, gently running a hand down the fur on her daughter's head. "How could I be so ridiculous?"

I paid attention to the spoken tone, volume, and body language between the two and couldn't help but find myself entertained. My children had never been this excitable at this age. This was my first experience with a human youngster, but I wondered if they were all so energetic.

"Crows are really smart," Georgia said, turning back to me. "I mean, they're *nonsapient*, but they do things that make them as smart as me! Like figuring out problems and using tools and recognizing faces. They remember if a human is nice or mean. You could feed the ones in your backyard fruits and eggs and nuts and seeds and build yourself a whole crow army!"

"An army?" I managed. "What for?"

Georgia stopped bouncing. "Like…security guards! They could make noise if someone's walking up to your house. And they like shiny things, so if they find, like, gold and silver and diamonds they'll bring them back 'cause they love giving you presents."

"On the other hand, we have a doorbell, and most shiny things they might bring you would probably be jewelry that people were wearing," Marilyn pointed out. "So maybe it's for the best that you can't build a crow army."

"No, I'd make sure they know not to steal," the little girl stated, folding her arms. "They'd have to go to jail and that's not fair. They're just birds."

I cocked my head. "I think technically the leader of the army would go to jail."

Georgia looked up at me and her eyes widened, and her mouth opened in a comical expression. *"Oh."*

Marilyn made a bubbling sound that my translator let through as laughter. "Oh, you must have children to come back with that so quickly."

"I do. Five, actually. And at this point I've given up counting my grandchildren."

"Oh my god," Marilyn said. "We struggle with one. I always say I have no idea how parents manage more than two."

"Oh, that's easy, you just lower your standards," I replied breezily. "After the third one, as long as you don't need to go to the hospital, an injury isn't serious. Then by number five, nothing is ever clean again."

The human laughed loudly. "That sounds about right. We need to go, we've got an appointment, but it was great to meet you."

"I'm sure I'll see you again soon. Georgia can come over and tell me more about your avians and keep telling me how beautiful I am," I said with a nod.

Marilyn stifled a chuckle and nodded. "Perfect. Come on, sweetie."

"Bye, Ackla!"

"Goodbye, Georgia," I replied. I watched them walk down the sidewalk toward the main street to catch the bus. "Well. Only danger so far is running low on oxygen because of their kids. Wow."

With my grocery basket full of all five things on my list, I walked toward the counter and got in line. Considering the wide range of products from different species, all the stores on the planet specialized, even grocery stores particular to types of food. The one I was in now was just for meats, and I'd picked up several kinds that were edible for me, one that I'd been craving that I planned to make for dinner. Most would go in the freezer.

The automatic doors at the front opened and the Niltonian at the counter named Molti, the owner, looked over to glance at his latest customer. His cephalopod eyes dilated and he raised one of his appendages at the Ankili that had just walked in. "No. You, out. I'm not selling to you Ankili garbage anymore."

The customer took a step back and looked around at the other customers, who were staring in shock, before he seemed to droop a bit, turning and leaving. I cringed in comprehension. I'd been watching the news last night and knew what that was about. *What a jerk. He's just trying to buy some groceries.*

"Whoa, hey, I'm sorry, what was that about?" stammered the human who had been putting their items on the counter.

"The Ankili president back on their home planet," I spoke up as I motioned in the direction the customer had left, drawing the human's gaze and that of their offspring. The youngster looked older than Georgia by a fair bit, but appeared to be the other human's child from similar features. *Both have short hair. Male until proven otherwise, I suppose? Ha.* "He gave a speech about Niltonians. A rant, more like. It's been on the news. Everyone's upset."

"Wow. You xenophobic asshole," chuckled the young human, staring at the store owner.

"Excuse me?" Molti exclaimed.

"Roger," the elder human said in unison. The younger one, Roger, cocked their head slightly, and the two seemed to have a brief back and forth using only their facial muscles. "Yeah…I guess." *Wow, that's a talent. I can say a lot with my feathers, but they just use faces.*

"He going to apologize?" Molti asked.

The human continued to take the last of their items from the cart and put them on the counter. "Are you kidding? I'm not going to have my son apologize for telling the truth." The Niltonian flinched. "You're telling me that if some leader back on Earth, some person I've never met, on a planet I've never even been to, says something bad about your species, I get kicked out of your store?" He snorted, shaking his head. "No thanks. Come on."

The two humans started for the exit.

"Hey, you're not buying any of this?" Molti snapped.

"Are you stupid?" the human replied, turning back to him. "I'm finding another store for meat. I give it a day before the news broadcasters here find some idiot politician back on Earth saying the same stuff. Oh, and don't worry, I'll leave a *thorough* review online about your policy of taking your chances shopping here. Maybe calling ahead to check how you feel about their species at the time."

The human shook their head as their offspring laughed and the automatic doors slid open to let them out.

"Human leaders on Earth are going to agree with that Niltonian jerk? Good riddance. Can you believe what just happened?" Molti asked, shoving the items to the side and meeting my gaze.

I blinked, glancing toward the door, and then dumped the contents of my basket on the counter. "Actually, yeah. I can." Turning around and ignoring his shocked face, I left the store, basket in hand.

Looking down the street, I saw the humans at the end of the block, the younger on his communicator, presumably looking for a new meat store. I made my way toward them. There was another good one just three blocks away that I'd tell them about. I'd only started coming here last year anyway because it was new and closer to my house. *Maybe I'll go online and leave a thorough review of my own.* I rustled my arm feathers in amusement.

Ohana Means Family

When I decided to major in xenoanthropology, it pretty much went without saying that I wanted to go to a university on Earth. They had still been staggeringly divided when they joined the Galactic Union, and there were an incredible amount of different cultures even on the same landmass. Borders didn't mean the same thing they had meant 200 years earlier, but pride and enjoyment of everything in your culture doesn't just disappear. Far from it.

Even after making time to read books and watch movies about American colleges, my first two years were an *experience*. I'm a Zalkinian, or Zalk for short, and our species tend to have a lot of children compared to humans. We're talking two dozen or so (don't worry, there are four parents to keep everyone alive!). So, it was pretty similar in college dorms.

One of the best things was that you were assigned a 'roommate'. Just one, but it was better than nothing. I hadn't realized how much I counted on the small noises of my sisters to comfort me and send me to sleep until the first night my roommate didn't come back until way after I'd gone to bed. And the dorm itself had many rooms on each floor, with shared showers and common rooms. That helped with the culture shock.

There were few students from off-world compared to the amount of humans, so it wasn't a surprise that I got a human roommate. Freshman year, the girl was outgoing and sociable, often staying out late. I didn't run into any big problems with her, and we became quite good friends. Sophomore year was a little more difficult. The girl assigned to share a room with me took a while to adjust to my appearance. She apparently wasn't fond of Earth's bugs, and I'm insectoid. But after a month or two of having lots of conversations, she adjusted enough to become friendly with me.

My third year, I decided to get a room off-campus, in a house with three other girls. It was a good start to gradually adjust my mind to the idea of having my own place. Especially since the others often had their doors closed for privacy. We still only had two bathrooms though, and mealtimes were often shared for convenience. One of us would make dinner for all of us, which saved time and money.

Aside from Kelsey. She joked that she could burn water and needed to spend months practicing her cooking skills before she was confident in her abilities. Often when it was her night to cook, after she made the attempt, we ordered delivery.

Kelsey was my favorite, because we got along so well but also because she was a film major. She recommended several movies to me right away, older movies that weren't well known, when I asked for recommendations to learn about Earth cultures. Then she asked if I wanted to watch some old movies with her about aliens, made before humans had met any. That was a hard *yes!* We set aside a Saturday to binge three and order Chinese food, splayed out on the large, wraparound couch.

The first one we saw was called Attack the Block, and it was both funny and emotional. Human films were quite good at combining multiple genres. I knew a lot about the history of Britain and the British empire by this point, of course, so it was fascinating to see a story about real, genuine characters who were average people in recent history. And who immediately killed an alien when it crash-landed near their block, a mistake that resulted in all kinds of trouble.

Then we went for 'infamous horror', as Kelsey put it, and watched Alien. Let me just say, when humans do horror, they really go all-out. I was sure I'd end up with at least one nightmare about facehuggers. Apparently, this film had a huge cultural impact, which did not surprise me at all, spawning a bunch of sequels. The dynamic of the crewmates, the terrifying chest-bursting monster, even the presence of a cat, everything contributed to an incredible film. Kelsey said we'd watch Alien 2 at some point also, which I both dreaded and looked forward to.

Before each film, Kelsey had skimmed the summary online to make sure there weren't any important cultural references I would miss, since I wasn't from Earth. The last movie was Lilo and Stitch (a nice animated film to cleanse the palate after Alien, she explained), and she showed me where Hawaii was, also taking a minute to explain its history and culture. That was important right off the bat, since I was able to enjoy the hilarity of Stitch's ship managing to land on the tiny spot of land in the huge ocean.

Surfing was something that I hadn't known much about, though I had vaguely recalled seeing a video clip of it at some point. Kelsey showed me some amateur footage of that. I was also given background on the musician Elvis, and she pulled up an old video of him on stage. Lastly, she covered the uncommon but well-known human concept of older siblings adopting younger siblings if their parents died, as well as 'foster care'.

I immediately knew I wanted to research more about that later, but I had no idea how important it was.

Stitch was a riot, a chaotic, entertaining, and *smart* troublemaker. But the audience's bond was primarily focused on Nani and Lilo at first. Lilo was only six, a fascinating age for humans, somewhere that left her a child in all the important ways and yet knowledgeable about so many things. Or maybe that was just from my perspective as an off-worlder, it was hard to tell. Kelsey told me to turn off my translator during the introduction, and I listened to the beautiful Hawaiian song that had been composed.

Comedic moments broke the tension constantly, but it didn't at all detract from the heart of the film, which was the concept of family. I learned Lilo and Nani were all each other had. Wonderful David, Nani's crush, was there to support them, but it was just the two of them in that house. A house where they had grown up, and where they now found themselves alone. Where Lilo despaired at being an outcast, listening to the lyrics of a solemn Elvis song.

> *...You still can find some room,*
> *For brokenhearted lovers to cry away their gloom*
> *You make me so lonely, baby...*

> *Lilo! Do you not understand? Do you want to be taken away?*

> *I shouldn't have yelled at you.*
> *We're sisters. It's our job.*

Nani, listening as Lilo wishes for a friend and, little do they know, will receive one that will change the course of their life. Stitch causing problems at Nani's job, having been literally created for chaos. Getting her fired. Throwing a tantrum and Lilo gently placing a lei around his neck, prompting him to plop down on the ground, bemused. The story of the ugly duckling.

> *What must it be like to have...nothing... Not even memories to visit in the middle of the night?*

And then David after Stitch is attacked while surfing. *You know, I really believed they had a chance. Then you came along.* It wasn't even his fault.

That's us before… It was rainy, and they went for a drive. What happened to yours? I hear you cry at night. Do you dream about them? I know that's why you wreck things and push me. Our family's little now and we don't have many toys but if you want, you could be part of it. You could be our baby and we'd raise you to be good. Ohana means family. Family means nobody gets left behind, but if you want to leave, you can. I'll remember you, though. I remember everyone that leaves.

I didn't even notice when I folded my legs under me. When the movie started to be more than a movie. When my breathing grew shallow and tired and sorrowful. Then that brief reprieve when David finds Nani a job, until everything goes horribly wrong.

You're not taking her! I'm the only one who understands her! You take that away, she won't stand a chance! She needs me!
Is this what she needs? It seems clear to me that you need her a lot more than she needs you.

No. No, the man was wrong, they needed each other. And they needed Stitch.
The abduction. The rescue. The councilwoman showing up, ready to take him away. And then…Stitch speaking slowly and deliberately…

This is my family. I found it all on my own. It's little and broken, but still good. Yeah. Still good.
This creature has been sentenced to life in exile, a sentence that shall be henceforth served out here…on Earth…and as caretaker of the alien life-form, Stitch, this family is now under the official protection of the United Galactic Federation.

My arms wrapped around me, I stared with unblinking eyes at the happy ending as they started to rebuild their house. Their home. Their new family. Jumba and Pleakley even stayed to help because, of course, they're family now too. They're ohana.

"What did you think?" Kelsey asked, turning the volume down as a song played by, I'm assuming, Elvis. She turned on the table lamp. "…Ch'Par?" she asked softly. "Are you okay?"

My body language was different from humans, but after living together for a while, the others had easily picked up on it. My arms were folded tightly over my chest. I felt that my eyes had faded from their bright green to something more ashen. And my antennae were drooped forward, completely limp.

"It was…wonderful," I whispered.

Kelsey hesitated and I saw her shift under her blanket out of the corner of my eye, still watching the characters bounce around with wood and nails on the roof of their house. "It was." She fell silent for a long moment. But as the silence stretched and I glanced at her, I realized she wasn't going to speak. She was giving me time until I was ready to do so.

"My family is small," I said quietly. "My mother… She had a small brood, just me and my two sisters. When they first realized how few she was having, they did a thorough examination and realized she was sick. It was something treatable but…not curable. She died when I was eight."

Pausing, I took a breath, unfolding my arms and clasping my hands together. "My sisters and I were always close, but we were so different in little ways. We never bonded like siblings typically do. And my father couldn't bear the idea of finding someone to replace my mother. Usually after the first brood, two couples bond to form a larger family and grow from there. But a year passed, then another, and eventually I realized it was just going to be us.

"That was fine. But it made us outcasts. We weren't mistreated, but it was like…others didn't know how to act around our family. The most important part of who we are as a species is usually building a family. Some people do only have one brood, and some even prefer to live on their own. Progress as a society made that acceptable as centuries passed. But…" I took in and let out a deep breath. "But this wasn't what we'd wanted. We were too small. Pieces were missing. We were… We were *broken*."

Kelsey's eyes had started to tear up, I saw, and she blinked rapidly a few times.

"We never fixed it," I murmured. "It was always enough, so we just went about our lives. And my father has started to talk about looking forward to when we start our own families, which is a big step for him. He sees the future, we see the future, and losing my mother is part of who we are, but it's not all of who we are." Kelsey nodded.

"But Lilo's family…" I met her gaze. "They were mending themselves with outsiders. Nani and Lilo, once they got through their struggles and steadied themselves, David was already becoming part of their family. They got Stitch and, like a dog, he was part of their family. You humans do that all the time with your pets. And Jumba. Pleakley. They just…brought other people into their orbit. Does that happen a lot on Earth?"

"Yeah," Kelsey said quietly, nodding. "It's called 'found family'. You ever heard the term?" I shook my head. "It's particularly valuable and treasured by humans who are different, even strange, or if they left the family they were born into because of abuse. Family is a profound word; it references those you're related to, but it's also the people you choose. Humans value connection, and we make many friends over the course of our lives, but at some point…that relationship can go beyond friendship. Saying someone is your friend isn't enough. It doesn't encompass what you mean to each other. So, you call them family."

I sat quietly, watching the credits roll on the film, letting my churning emotions gradually calm. Some color came back to my eyes. Then I looked to Kelsey. "Can we watch it again?"

Karen Avizur

Potential

Jackie looked across the sea of blue caps and gowns, everyone listening to the principal of their high school give his speech. She found herself wondering how much of it was identical to the year before. He probably couldn't get away with that. All the parents wanted their kid's graduation to be unique, to be *special.*

"And with that being said, I'd like to invite valedictorian Jaqueline Hart up to the stage," he concluded. He took a step back as the audience applauded, watching Jackie stand and walk up to the podium, her tablet in her hand.

Adjusting the microphone, since Jackie was a few inches shorter than the principal, she briefly turned away to clear her throat. "Good afternoon to all the parents and teachers here to celebrate my graduating class. I want to deeply thank everyone who supported me through my academics and extracurriculars." She paused. "I was told a valedictorian speech should, at most, be two pages. That won't be a problem. Because that was my speech."

Jackie smiled but didn't hesitate at the confused, soft murmuring she heard. Even her parents hadn't known about this. She watched as Izkar pushed the lever on her wheelchair's handle, wheeling her to the disabled access ramp up to the stage. "I'll be yielding the remainder of my time to a friend of mine, Izkar." She glanced to the left, where she saw Harry and a bemused janitor, whom he'd told about ten minutes ago that they would need a mic stand.

Izkar was an exchange student, one of fifty from three other humanoid species that had come from another planet for their senior year. She was Zalkinian, her structure insect-like, with two legs and four arms. Jackie's mind flicked through a few of the most memorable moments she'd had in the past year with Izkar, as well as the talk they'd had the day before, and was surprised at the emotion swelling in her chest. She swallowed it back to continue to speak clearly.

"The reason for this is pretty simple," Jackie told the crowd. "We attended the same school and many of the same classes. I may have gotten the better grades, but Izkar and I and our other friends thought she should be the one to give this particular speech. And we figured we'd just do it rather than complicate it with unnecessary things like asking permission. We are still technically in high school, after all." She heard some laughter as she removed the microphone from the podium's mic holder.

As Izkar stopped a few yards from the lectern, Harry was there with the mic stand, adjusting it to her height, as Jackie slipped the microphone into its grip. Harry headed back to his seat and Jackie gave Izkar a single nod of encouragement before following him.

"Hello everyone," Izkar spoke slowly, reading from the tablet on her wheelchair's tray. She spoke her native language, but of course everyone there had their translators hooked over their ears to hear it in the language of their preference. "My name is Izkar Hali. I'll be cheating today, because my speech is less than two pages, but I will still be setting a new record for longest speech." The girl was rewarded by chuckles from the crowd.

Izkar's spoken words were slow and deliberate because the translator needed to recognize what she was saying. Instead of the words stretching, of course, the translator left gaps between the words. But for her, this was not abnormal.

"When I first came to Earth to go to Nathan West High School, I thought it was going to be my biggest adventure. But I hope I was wrong, and I'll explain why. I have a disease that makes motor function difficult. Humans have something like it, called cerebral palsy. I talk slow, I move slow, and there are some things that are hard for me to do. I can walk around, but if I need to go a long way, like back and forth all day through the halls at school, I'll take my chair. And unfortunately, I'm not going to live as long as I'd like.

"On my first day of school, my mom asked who would be assigned to push my wheelchair from class to class. The principal was confused. He said, 'If you can't afford a mechanized chair, I'm sure the government will pay for one.' My mom asked who will take care of me through the day, though? The UN had told us my disability would be no problem, and any resources I needed would be provided. Who would bring my lunch to my table, we asked? Who would accompany me to the restroom?

"My mom and I were worried. We'd heard that humans were supportive of all its citizens with disabilities. But in that meeting, it felt like I wouldn't have any help, and I felt like my worries were being dismissed. But that was because we didn't know enough about humans yet.

"I got my mechanized wheelchair the very next day, one that was constructed for my skinnier, longer body shape. I went from class to class on my own, sometimes I took the elevator, and I went to the restroom on my own. And for lunch, there was a tray that slid up above my lap, so I could get my food and bring it to my table.

"There were a lot of students who were excited to meet me, and some of them became close friends. But they never really offered to help me with things. They were patient with me, though, and I got to talk a lot more than I thought I would. When I was younger, the other children were impatient. 'Just say it,' they'd tell me. And some of them were really mean, as we all know children can be. But my culture is quite focused on taking care of each other. So, my life hadn't been difficult.

"One day, a teacher of mine, Mrs. Monroe, called me over after class had ended. She mentioned that I hadn't been doing all the homework. I usually only did about half of anything I was assigned. But that's how it's always been, you see, because people assumed that was all I could do. I live my life in slow motion, even though my brain goes as fast as everyone else's. Back home, the lessons would be taught at school and then I would do some of the review problems for homework. But my Earth teachers said I should be doing all of it. Mrs. Monroe said, 'You're quite smart, Izkar. You should apply yourself more.' And she meant that I should do this for all my classes."

Izkar paused, looking to the section where her parents were seated. She could see her mother and father looking emotional. She moved her gaze away from them, not wanting to let her emotions overtake her and interrupt her speech.

"I felt overwhelmed. This was a new place with new people, and they expected so much from me. They didn't take care of me like everyone back home. But when I said that to Jackie one day, she explained that they didn't want me to push myself too hard. They didn't want me to strain and hurt myself and they didn't mean to give me goals I couldn't reach. They just weren't going to let me slack off. If there were fifteen problems on my homework, I was supposed to do all of them. Because I could.

"It wasn't insulting to me, saying that I was slacking off. It was just baffling. And it's only with hindsight that I can really understand what's different about humans. When I first fully realized it, I became so emotional. Because people at home took care of me, but it was because they thought I couldn't do it myself. Humans don't do that. Humans say, 'You need to do this differently? Okay, then. Do that.' It took longer, but that night I did all ten math problems. And I got it back the next day, in purple marker, graded a perfect ten out of ten. The first of many.

"By then, I was doing lots of other things by myself. I met with friends at the movies, and I bought and carried my own popcorn and soda. The public bus picked me up with a special lift for my chair, so I met friends in town all on my own. In school, I was assigned things to do in gym class instead of sitting on the side, and I even played dodgeball. But don't worry, I didn't get too much extra brain damage." There was startled laughter from the audience. Izkar smiled. Jackie had told her that one would get laughs.

"One day Harry asked me what I wanted to do after high school." Izkar stopped, feeling a swelling of warmth in her chest and she took a deep breath. "No one had ever asked me that before. Not like that. I told him I never really thought about it, since I'm not sure if I will even live to be thirty years old. Harry laughed and said, 'I could get hit by a truck tomorrow. I'm still planning to go to college.'" Izkar glanced at Harry when she said that, and he grinned back at her.

"Humans changed how I think about myself. There were times I was bullied, but even that was better, as crazy as that sounds. Because they treated me like any other kid. The worst bullying I experienced was when kids ignored me. Like I was a broken toy they didn't want to play with. Sometimes I felt invisible. Humans treat me like a real person. Like a *whole* person."

Izkar stopped again, taking a few breaths. "High school is hard. You're growing up and finding out who you are. But for me it was more than that. I found out my life could be bigger. My world could be bigger. And I found out that part of me *had* been missing, that I hadn't been a whole person when I first got here. But it wasn't because I was broken. It was because I hadn't realized I had all this room to grow. I couldn't see it. But my human friends always saw it.

"So, thank you. To all the teachers who knew I could do more. To all the students who always *saw* me. I'm going back home to tell my friends and family, 'I know who I am now. And I know I could still be more. And it's the greatest feeling in the world.'"

Karen Avizur

Sharing is Caring

Cultural exchange with other species is fantastic, as long as nobody accidentally says or does something that gives the other person the overwhelming urge to duct tape their mouths shut. Luckily, I work with 1ˢᵗ graders. I say 'luckily' mostly because they don't have access to duct tape. But I've seen them do damage with nothing but their bare hands, so it's always best to keep an eye on them.

We had just finished lunch and were having recess when I noticed one of the students, Rachel, skip from the playground back to where she'd left her toy and then come to an abrupt stop. There were three new students in my class, an insectile species, three Zalkinian siblings, and so far they had been doing surprisingly well in this cultural immersion experience. If you simply play up the awesome stuff about someone's home planet to human kids, and I'd started that on day one, you'd be surprised how far that will get you.

At the moment, however, Rachel was at a loss. She'd left a toy that she'd brought to recess unattended, and the Zalk kids had rushed over to check it out. I realized the situation immediately, and clearly her first instinct was to be polite, but she wasn't sure what approach to take. After a moment of wringing her hands, she walked over to them.

They spoke back and forth, Rachel pointing at the toy a few times, as the Zalk siblings put the spinning spaceship on the launcher, pulled the cord, and watched it fly off into the air and then fall. This happened several times and I finally saw Rachel look to me for help, shifting her weight from one foot to the other, her face pinched with anxiety. It would definitely escalate if I didn't intervene, though considering how it looked from afar, I really wasn't sure why it would be that serious.

Putting a smile on my face, I walked over as one of the Zalks, the boy, brought the ship back to the launcher in his sister's hand. "Hey everyone. Is that a cool toy?"

"It's awesome!" Kik exclaimed. "It flies! I never saw anything like this back home."

"Miss Brennan, they won't give it back," Rachel explained, pulling at her shirt.

"We're just having our turn," Lia told her teacher.

"Can I see the toy?" I asked, crouching to one knee on the grass. Lia didn't hesitate before handing it over and Rachel relaxed. *Ah, she's also worried they'll break it.* "It is very cool, but it's Rachel's toy. She brought it to school to play with, and you didn't ask permission. You just grabbed it as soon as she left it."

"But she was done," Kik protested. "It's sharing. Humans know about sharing."

"Right," I said. Pausing, I looked to Rachel and then back to the siblings. "And what is sharing?" I asked them.

Hiv finally spoke up. "Sharing is making sure everyone can have a turn!" she stated.

"Hm. I think I see the trouble here," I said, squinting for a moment in mock concentration. "Rachel, what do you think sharing is?"

Rachel hesitated, and I knew she was confused. This was an easy question, and also, the other child had just answered it. Or so it seemed. "Sharing is…letting someone else have a turn with your toy," she said slowly. "Or, like…giving a piece of chocolate to your friend."

"All right. So, you both have different definitions."

"What?" Rachel asked, glancing at the siblings and then at me. "No, sharing is…sharing."

"This is one of those *little things*," I said, emphasizing the words in the same way I had when introducing the kids to the class. "And because I am the teacher and I know *everything*," I exclaimed, producing glares and dry looks from my students, "I think I know why. So. Hiv, including Lia and Kik, how many brothers and sisters do you have?"

"Twenty-two," he replied easily.

"*What?*" Rachel shrieked. The siblings flinched in surprise. "How do you have that many? How old are they?"

"Um, we got three our age from my broodmother who are in another class," Hiv started, folding his fingers together and fidgeting, "and my broodmother also has a brood that are five years older than us. Then the other broodmother in our family, Hikral, her first brood are two years older than us and her second is three years younger." Rachel's eyes couldn't possibly widen any further and it was delightfully comical.

I grinned. "Rachel, you know how humans usually have one baby at a time, sometimes two, and more is rare?" The young girl nodded rapidly. "Zalkinians usually have five or six at a time. And they have two moms and two dads."

The girl gaped at me and then looked back to her classmates, flabbergasted. "Holy cow! How do you all fit in your house?" she asked.

"We…we got a big house," Hiv said, motioning with his hands. "How many siblings do you have?"

"I don't have any!" Rachel told them. "My mommy and daddy just wanted one baby." The three siblings were struck speechless for a long moment.

"But who do you play with?" Liv cried. "Who helps you learn stuff and-and…you sleep in a room *all alone?*"

"See, this is what I mean," I told them. "Little things like having lots of siblings versus no siblings make so many things different! When Rachel is at home," I said, motioning with the toy, "like other humans, she'll play with her toys, and sometimes have friends come over to play with her, and she'll share with them, because that can be more fun. When Hiv and Lia and Kik are at home, all the toys belong to everyone, because if they didn't, everyone would fight all the time. Right?" The Zalks nodded in unison.

"So…if you see a toy you want to play with, you just do?" Rachel asked them. "You don't have to ask permission?"

"There's no one to ask. All the toys belong to everyone," Kik told her. "But Mama and Papa taught us to *share*. I can't play with the balka ball for an hour all by myself, even if I want to. That's mean."

Rachel's face twisted curiously. I saw the brain cells working overtime and it was so sweet.

"So, you three have to understand, a human's toy is theirs, and you need to ask permission to play with it, or that's rude," I explained. "Maybe Rachel really wanted to play with this one toy for the whole recess. That's allowed. Or if you told her how excited you were and you thought it was awesome, and promised to be careful not to break it, she'd be happy to let you play with it the whole time until we go back inside. It's just her choice."

"Okay," Kik said quietly.

"We wouldn't break it. We'd be so careful!" Lia said, looking to Rachel. "We don't- If-" She paused, gathering her thoughts. "If we break a toy because we weren't careful, we get punished." Rachel blinked and stared in confusion. "Because then *no one* can play with it. And…there's just one of you, but there are a lot of us. Every toy is important."

"Which actually means they're super trustworthy if they want to borrow a toy," I pointed out to Rachel.

"Yeah," she murmured in reflective understanding. Rachel grinned suddenly, holding out the toy to the other children. "You guys play! I'll watch!"

They chittered excitedly. "Thank you!" Taking the toy from her hands, they set it up and pulled the string to make it take off. I smiled.

"Hey…can I ask you a question?" Rachel asked.

"Sure," said Lia, turning back to her.

"I've got a *lot* of toys, and sometimes my mommy helps me put things I don't play with anymore in a box to give to other kids. Could I…bring in some toys for you and Kik and…and Hiv?"

"Sure, that sounds great!" Lia exclaimed. "And you can come over to our house to play with us! It's got to be so boring playing on your own all the time."

Rachel nodded and smiled. "That'd be awesome!" She stared at the other kids, who were getting the hang of pulling the string just right to get the spaceship to fly higher, and beamed at the sight of them having fun.

The Battles in Epsilon System

Ghosts don't haunt the void. But at first, we weren't sure. When the first spacecraft was sent out into the black, a primal fear started to build. If the worst were to happen to someone, if a ship was vaporized, what would a spirit do if they didn't cross over? The ethereal was unknown on such a basic scientific level, even after all these years. It was something apparently not permitted for human knowledge, no matter who claimed to know for sure. Which meant we had no way to conduct any experiments to figure it out.

Any dead that were contacted had no information on the subject. People have often asked them what the afterlife is like, but during my sessions as a professional medium, I don't bother with clients interested in that line of questioning. The spirits who deign to respond don't have all-knowing powers. They are only themselves, and even describing them as such is giving them more of who they were and less of who they became. Death is not just a doorway; it's a transformation. To peace, to warmth, to love, to a way of being that no one can understand until you cross the Rubicon.

All conjecture seemed to assume that it was impossible for a ghost to haunt one spot in space. On Earth, there were no spirits that haunted areas several stories up just because a building used to be there. All of them found some sort of sanctuary, occasionally far from the place where they passed. So, it might have been hopeful thinking that allowed us to put aside our fears and leave for the stars without knowing the risks to our afterlife. But all the information we'd learned over the years concluded that if our spirits refused to move on for some reason, they would find their way to…somewhere. Somewhere with others. Somewhere they could be found.

The first deaths on spacecraft were from natural causes, and there were no signs of hauntings. Years passed as we continued to explore the solar system, then decades. Eventually there were hauntings, but even after all that time, there was not one spirit who was unable to be found, whether they'd crossed to the other side or stubbornly stuck around. Finally, we made the leap in scientific knowledge, the ability to cheat the rules and travel faster than light, and then the entire galaxy, the entire universe, was at our feet. As we had hoped, and expected, we were far from alone.

We learned that for a species to spread and survive in space meant a certain, new degree of cooperation and peace. But of course, even as it changed and we painted it as more honorable and civilized, war did not miraculously become a thing of the past.

Which brought me to this room. The HVAC humming, smelling of cleaning products and coffee and stale air, I was seated in a comfortable chair at a table for six. It was an invitation that was anything but, considering it was from NASA on behalf of Earth's off-world military forces, some light years away. They had called and I had arrived promptly on time in Cape Canaveral a day later.

They told me that a human colony planet, in a solar system of some value, had been claimed by another species and war had broken out. Everyone had known. The planet was not attacked; they attempted to invade, and we fought back. Everything was off-planet, resulting in minimal, if any, civilian casualties. But from the largest dreadnaughts to the smallest corvettes that flew and attacked in swarms, military casualties were the worst they had been for Earth in any war for over a century.

We won. But for me, back on Earth, that was just the beginning.

Epic Horizons: Tales of Human Greatness

The door opened only a few minutes after I'd sat down, and two men and a woman walked in, all smartly dressed, who each introduced themselves. I now only remember the name of one woman, Sergeant Major Laura Caldera, because she was the only one I spoke to after that.

They explained the situation, and I grew chilled.

There were many more injured, but the final count stood at 51,248 dead. The military had decided to contact me because I'd previously worked for them, so I'd already attained security clearances, and I had an overall near-unmatched level of experience. My straight, shoulder-length hair was completely gray, a daily reminder that I had lived, and indeed worked, more years than I had left.

"I've been assigned lead on this mission, and I'll be working to get you what you need," Caldera told me. "Billions of people are alive and safe in their homes because of the ones who fought in this war. But there were over 50,000 soldiers killed during the battles in Epsilon system protecting Seul. That's over 50,000 spirits, and some of the bodies will never be recovered. And we've been given the mission to make sure those soldiers are at rest."

Then she presented me with a check for $8.5 million.

"What comes next depends on you. What do you need?" she asked.

I opened my purse, took out my wallet, and tucked the check away. It felt vulgar to discuss my work with that extraordinary number in plain view. "Well..." I began quietly. After a few more beats, I answered. "I'm going to need help."

The money I was given was managed by my accountant, who had worked for me for about twenty-five years by that point. After my conversation with Caldera and the others, I talked to him over video chat to go over what we had mapped out at NASA. I made the plan and he budgeted to cut the checks.

The account of 51,248 dead was where we started, but the first matter of business was reducing it to the number of spirits who had not crossed over. Mediums that had been certified by national registries and also were governmental in some form weren't plentiful, but they weren't rare. Especially when you included Earth's population. After all, the spirit realm wasn't a place like a planet was, and you could commune with it on any planet, or indeed out on a ship in the void.

Only humans could be found on the other side, no alien species, and they all made their way there no matter where in the universe they'd been at their time of death. I knew that whether on Earth or Seul, many families and friends of the deceased soldiers would already be way ahead of us in trying to contact them. That was our first step.

Caldera put me in contact with a young man by the name of Matthew Wong, a military employee who I imagine had a job that consisted largely of making spreadsheets. He was assigned to our mission, and I gave him instructions, which he followed remarkably smoothly and quickly. Of those who had gone to mediums, he found that 11,982 had successfully contacted the spirit they had reached out to. Not all of them had the conversations they hoped for, of course; spirits are fickle things and sometimes the medium can solidify the connection but get very little in return. But we had confirmation on a certain number of souls. That left us with 39,266 spirits, location unknown.

My next step was to be a marathon séance. I called in three professionals I'd known for a long time, all with extensive experience. Michel Boisclair, Nazario Iadanza, and Mai Linh Chung. Nazario already had the security clearance needed, and the other two did the necessary excruciating amount of paperwork to do so. Then they flew into Orlando, met me at my hotel in Cape Canaveral, where they were all given their own rooms, and we sat down to discuss what needed to be done.

There had been hundreds of attempts to contact spirits that *hadn't* been successful, which were included in the list of 39,266 we now had. We would attempt those once again, along with the rest. That left 9816 (and change) for each of us. After beginning the séance, mentally conjoining our abilities to lean on each other when needed, we estimated dedicating a minute per spirit. A full minute to reach out and call across the other side of the veil.

Sixty seconds doesn't seem like a long time until you sit there and count it out. Especially for people at our level of talent, the fact that we only needed to determine the presence of the person meant it was plenty of time.

That came out to about 164 hours for each of us, to determine which spirits had managed to cross over. Food delivery and room service would be our saviors because mental work of this kind is exhausting when you're talking about working an eight-hour day (including an hour's break for lunch). We would have breakfast at the buffet, then order in lunch and dinner. That would give us time to get plenty of sleep, make use of the hotel's amenities like the pool and the gym, and have an evening discussion of that day's progress.

Two military personnel were stationed outside our room, not for security, but to ensure that we weren't disrupted. I insisted on calling them by their first names, Ella and Koby, and I got the impression they saw us as grandparent figures. Four older folks sitting around a table, not to be disturbed under penalty of, 'No dessert!' Each day we were texted when lunch was at the door and one by one we would end our session, and then a soft tone on my phone would sound after the workday was over and we ordered dinner.

We had all done lengthy séance sessions over the years, even some that required breaks, but nothing remotely like this. There wasn't much that was necessary for us to do the work, just a single (very tall) candle in the center of the table, so we could focus and meditate on the flame to help us get started. Well, two dozen of candles actually, since we switched out for a new one every day. Aside from that, I bought us four easy chairs; the ones the hotel supplied weren't sufficient to best support us through it all, especially at our age.

The estimate from the math was twenty-four days. But we knew that such ventures rarely stick to a schedule.

We'd come to the assumption that the vast majority of those who had died would pass on without issue, the same as those on any of our planets or in any war. This was important, because our schedule would go in the garbage if it wasn't true. We did have the statistics to go off of, from the other mediums who'd attempted contact of these spirits first, however. Several hundred misses out of over eleven thousand was quite promising. In that respect, it turned out we were indeed accurate, and as we began to go through our respective lists, we ended up checking off name after name.

The first few days went smoothly, and we got into a rhythm. Our eyes would close as we focused and reached for the deceased's spirit, not just with their name, but with several key words their loved ones had contributed. A soul is, after all, much more than a name. It's the entirety of one's being, many parts to a more valuable whole. Then we would put a check on a piece of paper in a pile in front of us or, on rare occasions, an X.

The positive results we received overall buoyed our emotions, encouraging us and letting us feel that it was a job that could realistically be done. Also, since we weren't attempting actual conversation, it was less strenuous work for each spirit than most of our jobs. After all, usually you didn't go to the trouble of contacting the dead unless there was something quite important you wanted to discuss.

Once we started to get into the second week, the strain started to become apparent. We began to go to bed an hour earlier, then two hours earlier. We became sluggish. Ella and Koby pulled rank (or rather, they called someone who could) and a physician was sent in to do basic checkups every evening after we'd finished our work. They would check blood pressure, pulse, and various other things that a military doctor could probably spot at a glance. But we also had a vial of bloodwork done and received recommendations to improve our diets.

Three days later, the doctor ordered Michel and me to take a day off. I wasn't pleased with the 'ordered' part; I would've taken a day if she'd asked politely. But I suppose in her line of work, it usually saved time to declare that there would be no negotiations. So, we did as we were told. Both of us took a nap in the afternoon for some extra sleep and spent a nice long time in the hot tub. Two days later, the doctor gave the same orders to Mai and Nazario.

The break refreshed us, it was apparent in our checkups and how we felt waking up each morning, but we were still sleeping two hours more than normal. The doctor wasn't exceedingly concerned about that, but she did keep painstaking records on our sleep schedule. She went so far as to give us a smart watch and small gadget to place on our bedside table that would know how we were sleeping from sound and movement. Every time I tossed and turned, it would take note.

Into week three, we started to feel the weight of exertion. The first morning I woke up and felt it, I became frustrated. Despite knowing the incredible level of my talents, despite how much we had accomplished so far, I was disappointed in myself. I suppose I had thought after a lifetime of training, this would simply be a challenge, not a real struggle. But I suppose, while I'd known my body's energy was what allowed my brain to do the work, I hadn't thought I would wear out so quickly.

Michel was the first to have different sort of troubles. He mentioned nightmares, the vague sort that leave you as soon as you open your eyes but are remembered because you know you haven't slept well. The day after that, he tapped out, as it were. Koby called in the doctor, who was staying just down the hall, and after a checkup, Michel was sent back to bed. Mai was the next to admit to nightmares, and there was no hesitation before putting her on bed rest as well.

That night, before heading to bed, I sat out on my balcony and looked out onto the ocean. I listened to the waves crash on the shore, breathed in the soothing salty air. Looking up to the stars, I wondered which of them were Epsilon. Ella had pointed it out to me, but I'd forgotten. Too many dots, even with the light pollution, to be sure.

The next day, I woke up from a distressful sleep and let out a long sigh. Sitting on the edge of my bed, I let my brain slowly wake up, I took a shower, and then called the doctor.

Each of us was prescribed five days straight of vacation. "You're no longer working for the government, as far as I'm concerned," she said cheerfully, having gathered us all in my room. "You have five days off and you are in a popular vacation spot. No excursions, but don't let your brain atrophy either. Watch interesting television, read books, take some laps in the pool. But also nap, enjoy the jacuzzi, and relax in the shade outside."

It was the first time I'd been ordered to take a fully paid, all-inclusive vacation. And yet, I wasn't exceedingly happy about it.

I spoke to Caldera that night and she told me sternly, "I know you want to help these soldiers find peace as soon as possible. But the key word there is 'possible'. I don't think humans have ever attempted something of this magnitude before, and I'll be damned if you slip into a coma from overworking your talent. The spirits may be unsettled and unhappy, but they aren't going anywhere, and I won't rush this. It takes as long as it takes."

Of course, she was right. It didn't make me feel any better, though. Every time I'd gone from one name to the next, to the next, to the next, and then had that rare moment of emptiness across the veil, that was one spirit suffering. Having given everything of themselves, they were now out there somewhere, unable to move forward for a reason we would need to determine.

Five days later, we were back to only needing one extra hour of sleep, and whatever the doctor saw when she did our checkups, it made her smile.

Less than a week later, we were done. Ella and Koby joined us for dinner down in the hotel restaurant. We each splurged on something that wouldn't have been approved by our diet regimen, and then got dessert to go. Sprawled around my room, my three friends and I had an evening that was essentially one long exhale. We'd begun with 39,266 names. We were now down to 143.

That number, though, had embossed itself on the inside of my eyelids. One hundred and forty-three souls lost somewhere. Scared? Angry? Confused? Bored? Who's to know? And where they had ended up, where their spirit had decided to flee to for reasons unfathomable to us, no one could guess.

It was at this point, with a manageable number, that Caldera reached out to each next of kin. The consensus my colleagues and I had reached was that a personal connection would be most likely to elicit a response. If their loved one was indeed on the other side of the veil, but just reluctant to reach back toward us, a long, patient séance by a skilled medium could draw them out. So, Caldera let them know that the military would be picking up the tab and gave them the name of the closest certified medium.

Unfortunately, the number did not decrease very much. Six souls were indeed on the other side and had needed encouragement and the voice of someone familiar to make themselves known. But that still left us at 137.

I had my friends, though. Michel, Nazario, and Mai were still pursuing this undertaking with me, and that meant thirty-four spirits each, with one extra. I took the extra, of course. Then it was the matter of finding them. I've done this before, if a client had asked for a loved one to be contacted, starting the session assuming that they had crossed over and ending up wrong. That obviously distressed them and so a search would begin.

Karen Avizur

About eighty percent of the time, I would estimate, the spirit was still in the home. Home is an instinct, something primal, and that intuition stays with the spirit even when so many smaller things have dissipated from their memory. Behind solid walls, behind locked doors, they were safe, and so they would retreat there without the conscious thought of doing so. Sometimes they became more aware of themselves, and sometimes they would simply become part of the furniture.

The other twenty percent of the time was a mix of obvious and not so obvious places. I've found spirits in schools, if that was their safe place because home was a nightmare. Some retreat to their favorite 'spot', like a bench in a park or even a frequented restaurant. But rare cases could have them end up at one place at the bottom of the list that the family only guessed out of desperation.

Matthew Wong, spreadsheet professional extraordinaire, gave me a call the next day and told me he mapped out the ideal route for each of us to take. Home to home, person to person. We were each assigned our three-dozen next of kin. He told me that 58% of them were on Earth and 42% on Seul. I'd been surprised, expecting more on Seul, but then again, Earth had a much bigger population and contributed many more soldiers to the military.

Since we guessed Seul was the most likely to have military personnel that would haunt unusual places, including military ships, my twenty-five percent of the spirits were all there. As the second-most experienced medium, Nazario took the rest, as well as some from Earth, and Michel and Mai had all Earth residents.

I'll admit it now. I was born on Earth, grew up on Earth, and had never even visited Seul.

By this point, warp technology had been streamlined. There are far fewer deaths from inter-system craft than planes, actually. When I compare it to taking a plane as a child, there isn't much difference. The seatbelts have more straps, but I'm doubtful that matters. When you're comparing turbulence at 35,000 feet and hitting a meteor when going thousands of miles per hour, I don't think a better seat belt is going to be much help. I figured it was more of a comfort thing and tried to put it out of my mind and trust in the engineers and mechanics.

For structural reasons, we're told, the craft doesn't have windows, but people hated that. They hated it to such a degree that there were significant anxiety issues and many people refused to travel on them. So, they found a workaround: tiny cameras on the outside of the craft that project to a small screen that imitates a window. I must say, it was incredible. The cameras shut off during take-off, warp, and landing, but everything it showed was crystal clear.

My breath caught in my throat when I first saw the galaxy spread across the sky while we traveled toward the warp point. And when Seul came into view, pure awe spread a chill down my back and goose bumps across my skin. I was so focused on it that when the video image disappeared as we closed in to land, I visibly startled.

We then made it back to solid ground, a process that, in comparison to air travel, did admittedly take quite a bit longer, as our takeoff had. Once we were given the go-ahead to disembark, I could tell the veteran travelers from those like me, still dazed from the experience. I was met by a military officer named Sergeant Park Liao, picked up my luggage, and went to my hotel.

The next day was more travel, this time by plane. In fact, I feel like I traveled just as much as I worked over the next few weeks.

Perhaps unsurprisingly, Seul was architecturally very similar to Earth. Humanity had gone with what we'd already known, after all. Some of the areas I visited were quite diverse compared to what I was used to, modeling off of other countries, but aside from that, it didn't feel much different. I was reminded of that every time we passed a McDonalds or a Starbucks.

One thing about being a medium that I haven't mentioned is…well…the living people I interact with. Many clients understand my limits, know the process (the Galnet is available to all), and are more curious than anything. But there are those who are impatient. Some are angry. Some work with me only to be let down, expecting a less complex process that's more straightforward and guaranteed. On Earth, I sometimes took difficult jobs, but I knew I could always walk away if it genuinely became too much, as rare as that was.

This was different. I'd agreed to do this job. I'd been paid more money than I'd earned so far in my life. And there were spirits out there who deserved rest more than anyone. There was no walking away if someone was being difficult.

Sergeant Liao turned out to be a huge help in that respect. Whatever his function in the military, clearly he'd taken classes in diplomacy. He had a soft smile, but when the occasion called for it, his face could lock down as if carved from stone. Liao knew what we were there to accomplish, and we were not doing it for the next of kin. We were doing it for the dead.

The first client is easiest for me to remember because it marked the start of the journey, and also because the deceased was a wife and mother. The family I met was her widow Adam and their ten-year-old son Benjamin. Corporal Amy Johansen was the spirit I'd need to find, and I saw photos of the happy family on the walls as soon as I walked in.

Staring at one that had been taken at a park, Adam walked up to my side. "That was last year," he said quietly. "It all happened so fast. The invasion, the declaration of war. Hugs and kisses goodbye. She didn't act like she wouldn't be coming back. None of us mentioned anything like that. It was all about saying we loved each other, her promising to be careful and not be a hero." He paused. "But she also didn't make any promises. She knew better than that."

Nodding slowly, giving one last glance to the bright smiles of the married couple and their son squeezed together for a photo, I turned and sat down in a loveseat. Across from me, Adam and Ben sat on a couch, serious, sad looks on their faces. Sergeant Liao stood off to the side, present and paying attention but purposefully out of the way.

"Okay. Give me just a moment." I shut my eyes and focused.

The best way to describe a search for a spirit in my presence is bat radar crossed with an awareness of signs from my body that something in the air is shifting. Like a cool breeze from an open window, a waft of heat from a fireplace, or a change in air pressure.

"Think about how much you miss her," I murmured.

That was no challenge to that, I knew. Likely it didn't even need saying. But it brought their feelings to the forefront of their minds, which was important. I concentrated, listening to my breathing, and then felt what I was looking for. A warmth drifted into the room, and I opened my eyes to see the familiar woman standing beside the couch, and my shoulders lowered as I let out a sigh. For her to manifest was no small thing. It was the strength that had gotten her home, and that had kept her here.

Depending on their mental state, some spirits can appear as they did when they'd died, while others look perfectly fine. Apparently, coming back home had settled her spirit to a certain degree, because she was immaculately dressed in her military dress uniform.

"Hello, Amy," I said with a gentle smile.

I won't go into the details of the next ten minutes. You already know what they entail. Private moments of a shattered family. Tears, despair, relief. The impossible conversation that consisted of explaining that Amy needed to leave, that staying here would damage not just her but her family. Repeating things that everyone had known before I had even entered their home, but I needed to say out loud to remind them.

They couldn't hear each other speak. They couldn't feel each other's touch. But once some time had passed, once everyone had let their emotions flow and said their final goodbyes, Amy released her grip on our plane and her soul slipped from my mind.

It never got easier over my career, having these conversations. On rare occasions, I needed to bring in backup if the spirit was violent, but from day one of this mission I'd doubted any of these soldiers would cause real problems. It took certain circumstances and, for the same reason the vast majority of the fifty thousand who had died passed on immediately, I didn't think it would happen here. Amy was the first to prove me right.

Returning to the car, I sat shotgun, Sergeant Liao and I shut our respective doors and he started the car. Then he sat there for a moment, long enough to draw my gaze.

"Is it always like that?" he asked.

I pursed my lips. Shook my head. "No."

"It's usually…less?" he asked, narrowing his eyes. "People who already processed it? This is just borrowed time?"

Letting out a long breath, my face went slack in comprehension. "No, Liao. It's not always this easy."

And it wasn't. Dozens of movies and shows over centuries have illustrated my talents. My career. They'll never run out of scenarios.

Some of the cases, many, in fact, went as Liao had expected. But not all. One soldier's next of kin was his sister, who he hadn't spoken to in twenty years. Another was the woman's wife, but they'd divorced last year. An older soldier, who had returned from retirement to be one more warm body on the front lines of the war, was a widow and had a complex relationship with his children.

People often believe that contacting their loved ones after they've passed away is that last chance they needed to say goodbye. They realize they regret something only when it's too late to rectify it. And some are relieved after I run a séance for them. But for some, even if they got what they believed they wanted, what they felt they needed, it falls short. It's not the same. I came to realize when I was younger that the veil separates us in a way we aren't built to comprehend.

The ones who don't attempt contact, I think they know that. It's a blurry, strange sort of secret, that even if we could explain it, we wouldn't. Death is a one-way trip to a place we don't know, and that journey, like all journeys, changes the soul. It makes sense that the ultimate journey would cause the ultimate change. But even knowing that, I have no idea what that means in any way I can describe. All I know is that it's my job to keep the machinery working, and to help get people to where they're supposed to go next. Anything more than that is beyond me.

We completed the easiest cases first, occasionally needing to visit other places nearby to find the spirit. Rarely did we need to reach out to a wider pool of friends of the deceased to figure out where they'd ended up. Luckily, though, this part of the job didn't necessitate blood pressure checks and unreasonable amounts of sleep. Often, public transport or even driving was an alternative to flying. After all, this was a planet of billions, but it was about the same size as Earth and still had a much lower population. And most of the population lived in the same areas.

Four soldiers were haunting ships; they'd been noticed, flickers out of the corner of someone's eye. Three of them were on-planet, one having made it to the surface in a crash landing, and the other two ships needed a more devastating term to describe their impact. Less landing, more crash. Then there was one that was in orbit, nearly dead, with only enough power for life support. The surviving crew had evacuated during a battle. Now a single woman remained, even though her body had been transported down to the surface.

"This is my first time on a warship," I spoke.

Liao looked over to me, both of us buckled into our seats in the small corvette that was currently docking. "Fourth, technically speaking."

I grimaced. "I don't think it counts when the majority of the ship is in pieces."

"Mm. Perspective, I guess." He glanced at his watch absently. "What was her name?"

"Layla Denovan. Corporal. She was twenty-one." I clasped my hands. "Same age as one of my granddaughters."

"I'll have to come with you," he told me. "Captain Griffin will manage life support, we've got a day's worth of time, but I've got to stay by your side. Safety reasons. This ship did just survive a war, don't forget."

"It's the only thing I can think about," I said, shaking my head.

Several lights went on, beeps sounded that meant something to Liao, since he unbuckled himself. I did the same, following him. He opened the airlock door, going through procedures that I'm guessing were second nature to him, and I stayed just two paces behind him. The ship had been double checked, damaged areas that were open to vacuum sealed off by multiple doors, and then Captain Griffin had done his own check to be sure. The ship was far from battle ready, but she was safe for us to walk through.

Liao checked his communicator. "This way," he said quietly.

Walking close behind him, I put my hands in my pockets. I'd expected there to be more noise. Creaks and groans like a ship at sea, or machinery clicking or clunking away in the walls. But it was startlingly quiet. Once I thought about it, it seemed obvious. Despite traveling faster than I could imagine, this wasn't an airplane, buffeted by winds. It was an unyielding force of strength and technology that managed to survive even when parts of it exploded, designed to move as if carved from steel.

"That was her bunk," Liao said, pulling me out of my thoughts, motioning in through an open doorway.

I walked inside, looking over the small bed built into the wall. Sitting down on the mattress, the first thing I'd heard that did creak, I looked over the blank wall, as opposed to the others in the room that all had photos taped up. When I leaned back, on a hunch, to look up at the ceiling just a foot above my head, there was one photo taped to it. Her in much younger years with another young girl of some relation, from the similar shapes of their faces.

Though Liao was still there, I saw him move to stand against the wall outside. Sitting up straight, I took a deep breath and let it out, relaxing my mind. "Corporal Layla Denovan," I called softly. Waiting in the silence patiently, attentive to any changes, after a minute I let out another breath. "Corporal Layla Denovan," I spoke again.

There it was. A chill that breezed across the room. I opened my eyes and didn't need to look far. Just three feet away, she stood staring at me.

A large shard of metal was embedded in Layla's stomach, blood covering the left side of her body, revealing she'd bled out and died where she'd fallen. She stared at me, unblinking.

"It's time for you to go," I whispered to her. "The war is over."

Pausing, Layla walked stiffly to the bed across from hers, as if she could feel a coldness I was immune to, and carefully sat down. "Who are you?" Her voice was quiet and rough, but somehow still strong.

"My name is Deborah Marciano. I'm not military, though I was given clearance to help you. You and many others."

"How many others?"

I knew what she was asking, and it wasn't how many ghosts I'd spoken to. "…The final count of deceased was 51,248."

Layla lowered her head, breaking her gaze with me. "It wasn't supposed to happen. Not like this. Not right away." She paused, but I didn't fill the silence. "We came so far…did so much… And still, we couldn't fly fast enough or far enough to get away from war. It was supposed to be better here."

I knew Layla's background. Raised by a single parent, her father. Intelligent enough to alienate her from her peers. Determined enough to join the military. Young enough to think she lived in an age of better things, and yet old enough to understand that the universe doesn't allow for perpetual peace. Old enough to be angry, but not surprised, when war came to her world.

"Was it better?" I asked.

She hesitated. "Yes. Better than a hundred years ago. Better than a thousand. Just not…not better enough."

I nodded my understanding. "Why are you still here?"

Her face showed no emotion as she considered the question. "I kept trying to keep going. Keep moving forward. Keep fighting. And I did. Until I didn't… And I'm not sure I want to anymore. I wanted to try staying in one place."

"I know what you mean." Pausing, I sat up straighter, clasping my hands on my lap. "Do you think you're ready to start moving again?"

Layla's pale eyes moved to meet mine again. "Is that an order?"

"I can't give you orders. You're former military now, Layla," I told her. That finally brought the first flicker of emotion from her. "You fought and you gave everything. That's what they asked for and that's what you gave." Her lips pursed in consideration. "So, I'm not ordering. I'm asking. Are you ready to start moving again?"

There was a long silence during which Layla kept her gaze on mine, during which I blinked a few times and she didn't. Then she slowly nodded. Pushing herself back to her feet, she turned to her left, and within a few paces, dissipated into nothingness.

After a few beats, I looked over to Liao. He raised his eyebrows in a slight twitch. I nodded. "We're done."

The Crash Site

The call came in at 15:48, sending my partner and me racing down the 441 in the back of our ambulance toward the farmer that had put in the call, Lenny Jericho. He had reported some sort of crash or explosion, and dispatch had advised us that there was something wary in his tone. Dispatch told Jericho to stay in his home and that the EMTs and police would investigate. At the moment, though, there was an unfortunate coincidence of a sizeable fire that the department was dealing with on the other side of town. Likely we'd be the first on scene.

The driver pulled the ambulance to a stop, and when we flung the doors open, I saw we were a few dozen yards from expansive stretches of corn plants stretched in all directions. There was a small plume of smoke gently wafting into the sky. Donnie and I leapt out, each with a bag of supplies slung over our shoulders, and he grabbed a fire extinguisher. Then we made our way quickly into the endless field of corn, guided by the faint smoke signal. When we broke through the rows of corn to the edge of a clearing, I realized it had been caused by a plane carving a gouge into the earth as it had crashed.

That was the last rational thought I had because the jagged mess of metal and cracked glass in front of me was not an airplane.

Donnie found his voice first. "Holy smokes," he breathed. "For real, Rosetta, what…what are we looking at?"

I stood stock still, taking in the incredible, massive craft. It must have been well over fifty feet from wing tip to wing tip and it looked like something out of a sci-fi movie. It was dark and sleek, like a cutting-edge craft that would be displayed and flown at a top-secret military air show. My instincts pricked the hairs on the back of my neck in apprehension, but my training took over and I shook my head, trying to clear the cloudiness that had smothered my thoughts.

All right, do your job, I thought.

"Donnie, there's got to be a door, but there's no way we're getting it open," I snapped. "Our best way in is a window."

"But those things have got to be insanely tough," Donnie told me, as he quickened his pace to match mine. We headed toward the wing tip that laid against the ground, which we could use to climb up toward the windows. Donnie stopped at a portion of the wing that had been giving off the smoke signal and hit it with a good, long spray with the fire extinguisher. Once it was completely smothered, we continued on. "You think we can get in?"

"Not sure, but one of them's already cracked, so we'll try that one first." I touched the metal with the back of my hand to gauge its temperature, but it was neither burning hot or icy cold, so I took a step onto the wing. Shifting my bag so it was tight against my back, I balanced warily on the steep angle as I took cautious steps. "We can try the glass-breakers if we have to, but hopefully the impact did enough damage to let us in with a few good kicks."

We reached what was presumably the cockpit and I noticed that there was significant damage to the larger of the four windows, the metal having warped to the point of dislodging it. "Here." I stomped hard on the glass and was relieved to feel the window give under my weight. "All right, help me out here." Donnie took a few steps to my side and we worked on the edges of the window, still unable to see into the darkened interior.

After a minute or so of that, a large piece of it crumpled away, dropping inside with a *clang*, leaving plenty of room for one of us to squeeze in. "Anyone alive in there? This is emergency services." I listened carefully but heard no response. I dropped to my knees, grabbing my flashlight from my belt, flicking it on and looking inside.

Sliding my flashlight across the interior, it landed on something. My brain hiccupped, flipping through damage that could reduce a human being to this appearance, and finding nothing. Then I jerked backwards and screamed, "Sh-sh-sh- What-what is…"

"What?" Donnie asked, on the verge of a panic at my reaction. "How bad is it?"

"I-I don't…"

Donnie grabbed his own flashlight and took a look inside, flinching violently at what he saw, but not as severely as I had, having had the preparation of mentally raising his guard. "What…" he stared. "Rosetta, what the frack is…"

I swallowed hard, but forced myself back to the window, looking down into the craft as every science fiction movie and novel I'd ever read came flooding through my brain. The closest thing I could compare it to was an octopus, but it had scales like a fish. The creature wasn't in a suit, presumably having not expected to crash land on our planet. That poked at my curiosity and I wondered why it was here, but that train of thought could most definitely wait for later. Vicious cuts from the crash were spread across its body, dripping red blood from the wounds.

It was moving. Struggling. It was alive.

"It's alive," I said, something numbing my brain to the extraordinary and settling back into the routine of my job. *No hope, no fear.* I clenched and unclenched my fists as I repeated the mantra, steadying myself. *No hope, no fear.*

"Who-Who do we call for this?" Donnie choked out. "Who- *Rosetta!*" he shouted as I dropped through the hole.

"It's alive, which means it can *stay* alive, Donnie!" I barked at him. "It's got red blood, which means it's probably oxygen based, but I don't know how long it can survive on our air."

"It's a fracking alien, Rosetta!"

"I got that part," I snapped, tilting my head up to meet his gaze. "You want to be the one to tell the CIA or whoever that we let it *die*?" He let out a shaky breath, lifting his hand to his forehead. "Get down here, look through the equipment, see if anything looks familiar. Anything that looks like it could fit over…" I looked back to the creature, not even sure if it was near death, but something had taken hold of my heart and I was desperate to ease its pain and keep it alive.

At that moment, it moved, pulling away from me, as Donnie lowered himself inside the craft.

"Hey, hey, it's okay," I said gently, carefully putting a hand against one of its smooth, scaly appendages. The large eye in its head slid to look at me and my heart skipped a beat, my vision going blurry for a moment. The part of my brain that was freaking out tapped me on the shoulder, telling me that an overwhelming flood of emotion was ready to pour out in whatever way I'd like at the drop of a hat, just give the word.

No hope, no fear.

We weren't hurting it; instead, we were taking some action. That would be unmistakable to the creature, or at least I hoped so. We were here to help and I wanted it to know that.

I pointed to my mouth. "Can you hear me?" I asked, not knowing if the creature had ears. I clapped several times, pointing to and tugging on my ears. "Can you hear me?"

The creature's movements were sluggish, but it managed to raise one of its tentacles to the side of its bulbous head, where I noticed an opening of some sort. Ears. It had ears.

Which left me with no strategy in terms of communication, but it was something, I guess.

"I found this," Donnie said, lugging over a metal canister-like contraption with a short hose leading from it to something plastic-looking.

I pulled it over to the creature's vision and clearly saw its eye dilate. "This means something," I told Donnie, meeting his gaze before looking back at the creature. I pulled it as close as I could, coaxing the alien to take the lead. Its movements were still slow and shaky, but it managed to get a grip on the canister and pressed something on its side that I couldn't see. The canister's gaseous contents spurted out with a jolt, startling both Donnie and me. He swore under his breath.

"This has got to be, like, an oxygen tank," I said. I helped the creature let a second tentacle grasp the plastic end that I was holding and pulling it under the lumps of its other appendages. If it were anything like an octopus, it would have a beak, but I was guessing that wasn't the case, since the rounded plastic contraption at the end wouldn't fit over a beak.

I waited anxiously for some sort of reaction. After barely ten seconds, color flooded into the creature's head, turning it from blue to more of a reddish-purple. "Oh my gosh. It was hypoxic," I breathed. "Or…what's the equivalent for… We don't even know what it breathes." As I watched it inhale and exhale, after a few times, I started to breathe in unison with it. *In…and out…in…and out…*

"I don't… Rosetta," he said. He licked his lips anxiously and swallowed hard. "What do we do now?"

My head shook slowly, my subconscious knowing before I did that that question had no answer. But then the creature's eye focused on me once more and it reached out with a tentacle, steadier this time, and gently grasped my hand. I wrapped my fingers around it in the best approximation of a handshake I could manage.

Centering myself, taking slow, even breaths as the alien did the same, I focused on staying in this moment as I heard the faint wail of sirens rapidly approaching. This quiet, calm, and wondrous moment beyond imagination. Because I knew that very soon, my world would be swept up in a chaotic tornado, and I had no idea if I would ever land back on solid ground.

The Dinosaur

It was about nine p.m. when I parked at the end of Harold's long driveway, turning off my truck and headlights and heading toward his front door. For almost three years now, Harold and two other work buddies of mine got together every Friday night for poker. It was for chump change of course, Harold's wife wouldn't have let him run a real game out of their living room, but it was good fun.

Halfway there, I noticed a light that had been left on in the barn. That wasn't that much of a concern to me, I'd let Harold know when I get inside that he'd forgotten to turn it off, but then something inside moved. And when I say something, I meant not a person. Harold had chickens, sure, but this was no goddamn chicken either. This was *big*.

I froze in place, my gaze moving back and forth from the house to the barn, before curiosity got the best of me. My feet crunching on the gravel driveway, I gradually made my way over to the small entrance door to the right of the larger barn doors. I paused, listening to the thing inside, and to be honest it sounded to me like it was chewing on something. A horse? A cow? That did it. I swung the door in.

My jaw dropped and I froze. A dinosaur. There was a goddamn *dinosaur* in Harold's barn. And I'd be damned if it wasn't wearing a saddle.

I should probably back up a bit at this point. We worked for a genetics research lab in the city and for ages, my buddies and I had heard water cooler chatter about bringing back extinct species. Like mammoths, letting them loose in the tundra, seeing how they could help balance the environment or something like that. This wasn't my specialty; I just mopped the floors. And enough time had passed that I'd guessed they'd made some progress, but this was DARPA stuff, way out of my league.

Or so I thought. I gulped back the fear rising in my throat, threatening to turn into a scream.

The dinosaur was chewing away at a giant pile of hay and, at my entrance, had turned to look at me, gazing with large, clueless eyes. There was no doubt about it, this was an animal with very minimal intelligence. And whatever instincts it had built-in to protect it from predators, clearly I looked nothing like something it should be afraid of. So, its jaw kept moving, chewing the hay, and eventually when it finished it bent back down to grab another mouthful. It then looked back up at me, cocking its head curiously.

I nearly leapt out of my skin at the hand on my shoulder, spinning around and gasping in a sharp breath. "Harold!" I shouted.

"Shh!" he hushed me, shoving me into the barn with a hand over my mouth. He shut the door behind him. "I saw your truck pull up, knew you were taking too long. Why'd you have to-"

"There's a dinosaur in your barn," I hissed. My hand went to my head. "We're dead. We're all dead, they're gonna find out what you did, and I know, so now I'm an accomplice-"

"Would you pull yourself together?" he exclaimed quietly.

I tried to do so, putting my hands on my hips and taking a few deep breaths. I then pointed at the creature. "Why's it wearing a saddle?"

Harold grimaced. "'Cause I been training it. For Maggie."

My eyes bulged. "You're gonna let your granddaughter on that thing?"

"It's an herbivore," he assured me, motioning to the hay with his left hand. "And I've been on Dino plenty of times to-"

"Dino?" I managed. "The dinosaur's name is Dino? You couldn't get more creative than-"

"It's from the Flintstones," he protested, indignant. "I loved that show."

My face fell into my hands and I rubbed my eyes for a moment before sighing. "Man, what were you *thinking*?" I whispered. "You're not just gonna get fired, you're gonna get *arrested*."

"For stealing a dinosaur?" he deadpanned. "I'm sure that'll go over well in court."

I shook my head in dismay. "Court? You know how these things go. You'll be dropped in a hole somewhere like Gitmo and prosecuted for treason for violating state secrets-"

"Look at her," he pleaded. "Just…look."

Pursing my lips, I sighed, then looked over to the animal. I understood the feelings behind Harold's tone. The creature was beautiful, in its own way, really magnificent. I hadn't had a chance to take it in among my panicking, so I did for a few long moments. "What is it?" I finally asked.

"Chilesaurus diegosuarezi," he answered.

"I'm not gonna try to repeat that," I said. "Trip over my own tongue, I would." Scratching the back of my head, I let out another sigh. "Does Betsy know?"

Harold looked at me like I'd lost my mind. "Does my wife know I've got a dinosaur I've been raising in our barn? Tell me, Charlie, you think you'd be able to keep a secret anywhere near this big from Cheyenne?" I nodded. *Fair point.*

"This is just the first outside the lab, you know," he said. There was something heavy in his voice. "They've got more, and they've got worse. Herbivores, sure, go full Jurassic Park, but carnivores? T-Rexes? People are gonna get killed. I saw those latest movies, and these guys are just as arrogant and stupid doing this stuff in real life, I can tell."

"People get killed all over the world every day," I said sourly, staring at the animal. "Dinosaurs won't change that one way or another. And even if they do, if they make it worse, we'll get used to it. There's always a change and there's always a new normal. You know that as well as I do." I looked over to him, one aging codger to another and saw the disappointment and reluctant agreement in his eyes.

"To be honest…I know this is gonna change the world, and I wanted…I wanted Maggie to be part of it, you know?" Harold asked. "And in a way that's beautiful instead of scary. She's gonna grow up in a different world than we did, man. There's change and there's…whatever's gonna happen in the next fifty years."

I grunted. "All right."

"All right, what?"

"I won't tell anyone," I said, looking to him. "Not the boys. Not even Cheyenne."

His eyes bulged. "Not even her? You mean it?"

I nodded. "One condition."

"Name it."

I took my cell phone from my pocket. "You get a picture of me on that thing."

The Human's Pet

To be quite honest, I was just as upset as the rest of the council when the human insisted on bringing an animal of another species, an unintelligent one at that, to the meetings. These were extremely formal proceedings, with traditions and customs that went back centuries. To disrupt all of that for one *pet* seemed outrageous. My colleague, another citizen from Savarie, was my partner in this, and he didn't understand the presence of the animal either.

Unfortunately, the human was one of two that had been elected to the council democratically. That was customary on Earth, and so there was absolutely nothing I could do about it, even as a head council member representing my country. So, in the end, we had an extra occupant in that room, around that expansive table. And I was stuck next to them. Even so, I still had no idea what the animal's purpose was, and it felt rude to ask.

Honestly, when I'd first heard rumors about the animal, I was terrified, though it was mitigated by the fact that I knew humans were a reasonable species overall. When I first saw the photo of the yellow-haired beast, I was concerned about the size, but it seemed, while walking on all fours, not to come up any further than the human's waist. Since I was only a little shorter than the human, that didn't make it ridiculously large. Yes, the teeth and claws concerned me, but the video that the human sent to all members of them playing together without the human being injured put that part of my mind at rest. I had no doubt these animals could be used to protect their owners, but it seemed this particular dog was…joyful, I think was the best word for it.

As the meeting wore on, the animal continued to be well behaved, curled up beside the human's chair for the duration. Despite my best efforts I became desperately curious of what the reason was for the male human's pet. The human had a female colleague, the other half of the pair of Earth representatives, so it wasn't that he needed company from home that was the issue. Also, I knew that interspecies mating was taboo on their planet too, so that eliminated that possibility.

I must comment here that it was quite adorable when, on rare occasions, the human subtly bent down to wake him when small, panicked squeaks came from his mouth, the result of a bad dream.

At the fifth meeting, the answers became clear. Or rather, a little clearer, since when the incident occurred, it prompted many more questions. The animal, strangely, had sat up and nudged the human with its snout. I wasn't familiar enough with human body language to read how the human felt about this attention, but he pet the dog a few times in the head. This happened several more times, before the male human's colleague leaned over and spoke to him.

"Shall we put it to a vote then?" asked Vitinu, a colleague of mine from a neighboring star system. His voice spoke into a microphone in front of him, translating into the earpieces of each species present. "If there are no other-"

That's when it barked, repeatedly. To say we were flustered was an understatement. Shock was the first reaction, then outrage, and voices started speaking back and forth immediately. I myself was irritated and insulted. There had been no warning that the human had given that the animal might do such a thing.

"I knew that creature wouldn't last long here!"

"That noise is unspeakably loud, make it stop!"

"Senior Counselor, can you order it removed from chambers?"

The human, however, did not look distressed in the way that I would have expected. He wasn't embarrassed and didn't move to hush the creature, only to stand up from his chair, leaning down to the microphone. "My apologies to the council, I appear to be experiencing a medical emergency." His voice managed to cut through the cacophony just enough to bring a hush to the crowd.

There was a brief moment where I heard the woman's voice echo through the microphone, "…told you not to put off her nudges, idiot…"

The man turned to the woman, nodding once in the direction of the door. "I request a brief recess, after which we can resume the meeting and go to a vote." The woman stood as well.

"Of-Of course," the Senior Counselor managed. "Is there anything we can do to assist in this medical emergency?" He seemed as confused as I was, since it appeared the human was fine.

"No, I just need to-" He stumbled and the woman caught him.

"You've got to lie down, it's coming on quick," she snapped at him, helping him down to the floor. He twitched and jerked. She gently turned him on his side, not restraining him, but helping keep him in place. I saw the woman reach into a bag she'd brought with her, taking out a pillow and placing it under his head.

The animal, the creature that had been subject of so much concern and anger, merely lay beside the man, almost at attention as a military officer would be. And I made a sound of distress as I saw what continued to happen. The human male's body lurched and spasmed. His eyes rolled back and closed, the female's hands gentle on his back and shoulder.

The room had gone deathly silent aside from the human's thrashings and hushed voices from those too far from this edge of the table to see what was happening. I noticed the woman checking something on her wrist, and after some examination I realized it was a small machine to tell time. I tensed. How long would this episode last? Could he injure himself? Could he die right in front of our eyes?

The Yuluti representatives seemed particularly concerned about this episode of illness, and I wondered if they had something similar that occurred for some in their species. The Reptilians were having a hushed conversation amongst themselves, and the Zalkinians were both on their communicators, presumably looking for information. The Minakans were the only ones that looked calm, only mildly concerned, and I wondered if they knew something we didn't.

Finally, the man's movements ceased, and his body relaxed. The woman slowly rolled him onto his back, speaking to him softly. He did not move or reply as she took out a communication device and spoke into it. Less than a minute later, the double doors at the entrance swung open and two human medics came in with a thin, padded cot. They quickly made their way over to the human, helping him off the floor.

Once seated, the woman turned to the dog, which had been standing by and keeping a close eye on the man, and she tenderly patted its head and rubbed it behind the ears. "Good girl," she said softly. My spirits lifted at the sight, and at the animal's tail, which had started wagging back and forth. A sign of happiness, I'd been told.

We watched in surprise as the medics carried the man out the door and my anxiety spiked, realizing the man still apparently couldn't be relied on to walk on his own. And, surprising me again, the animal walked patiently and attentively behind them, accompanying them out the door with no commands.

"It's what's known as a seizure," the woman explained into the microphone to her stunned colleagues. "They're quite rare for him, but we couldn't take the risk we would have one here and not know it was happening ahead of time. That's why his medical dog Lacy had to be here. Dogs can sense when a seizure is about to happen and alert the human. It's…a personal health problem, so he was reluctant to share it. But I suppose the secret is out now."

The Senior Counselor was the first to find his voice. "Of course, we understand. That is truly a fantastic gift his pet has, and I'll be doing some research on…what did you call it?"

"Seizure."

"Seizure. I'll ensure our medical personnel have my own personal account of what was experienced here to add to our emergency procedures. It looked terrifying. Will it cause permanent damage?"

She shook her head quickly. "Not for him. He'll make a full recovery, likely by the time we're finished here." I glanced in the direction the man had been taken. Full recovery? Back to normal after that? "There are different kinds, different levels," the woman explained. "Some people don't shake at all. And I'm sure most of your medics know procedures. Still, that's very kind of you."

"One thing I will absolutely make sure of is that assistance animals such as yours have no difficulties accompanying their humans to any governmental meetings," the Senior Counselor added with a decisive movement of one of his four arms.

The woman nodded. "Thank you. I'll tell him when I next see him. I'm sure he'll be very proud to hear how well Lacy performed her job and not at all surprised," she said with a knowing smile.

I decided that once proceedings were concluded, I would visit the human in his hospital to show my respect. Reaching this prominent post despite his condition had likely been a steep climb. Let it never be said that humans are weak, even in the face of something that has driven them to their knees.

The Humans on the Front Lines

Three.

The cameraman before her, José Orduna, counted down on the fingers of his left hand, his right holding his large camera. Yun Teng stood waiting patiently beside two Holkanitan citizens, who she had prepped for the interview. The last few days on-planet had been incredible, but it hadn't taken long for her to get into the same rhythm she always had. Her job had been the same for three decades. 'The war is the war is the war,' as her mentor had taught her.

Two.

A week earlier, Inpelato ships had shrieked down from the sky and flown across this part of the colony planet, a populated area with a strong military presence nearby. Several political targets had been taken out with missiles that hit city administrative buildings, and further, the hydroelectric dam had been blown to pieces. Power had been lost to over two million Holkanitan citizens, but worse, thousands had been killed in the immediate flooding. Many were missing, and they were struggling to tally the dead.

One.

This was Yun's first on-planet assignment for a war that had been going on for two years now. Earth's joining of the Galactic Federation was soon to celebrate its first anniversary, and those in charge had recently reached out with a request to send someone to the front lines. When her boss at the station had sat her down to tell her of their success, he had to clarify something, and amidst the incredible news, a strange expression had contorted his face.

"Just one thing. You're going to be the only one down there."

"I know. But I'll have José."

"That's not what I meant. Yun…the folks at the White House had to explain that we were sending you to the war. Not a Holkanitan ship, or to talk to Holkanitan politicians. Apparently, the conversation went, 'We want to send a war correspondent,' and their reply was, '…What's that?'"

José's finger flicked to point at her. *Go.*

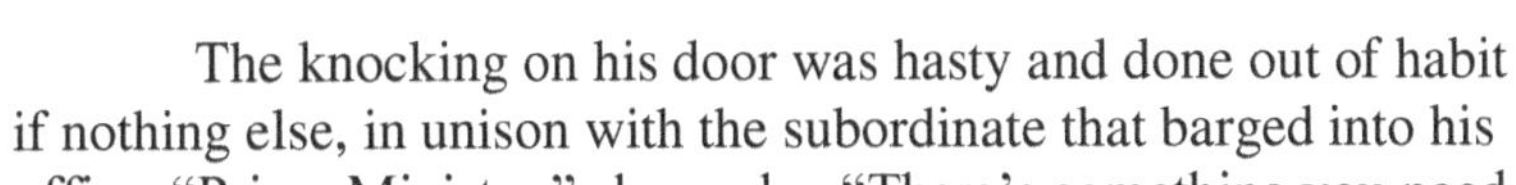

The knocking on his door was hasty and done out of habit if nothing else, in unison with the subordinate that barged into his office. "Prime Minister," she spoke. "There's something you need to see."

The Inpelatonian flicked his claws against the desk in a gesture of irritation, but didn't reprimand her. "Apologies," he spoke to the man he'd been speaking with. "If you'll give me a moment."

"Of course."

Prime Minister Palinit stood from his desk and walked quickly with the woman into the adjacent room, shutting the door behind them. "What in void's name was that about?"

"You need to see this." She walked around the large meeting table, over to the screen on the left wall, tapping to turn it on and then rapidly flipping it to view broadcast channels, selecting one. A voice filled the room and Palinit watched for almost thirty seconds, stunned, before speaking.

"What is this?" he asked slowly.

"It's an Earth war correspondent."

"Yes, I can see that," the Inpelatonian snapped, pointing a claw at the screen. "That's a Holkanitan citizen! Is this live? What in void's name are they doing on a Holkanitan colony planet, talking to some random citizen, *live*? They said they were unbiased, looking only for facts, the truth as we see it. And they said they were sending the reporter *here*."

"And they did," she told him. "I saw his work yesterday and he's talented." She pointed a claw at the screen. "This is not him. He is in Arko right now, and this one has short hair but is a female. We made a mistake. We thought they were asking to send *their* war correspondent to speak to our soldiers and civilians-"

Palinit interrupted. "That's what they did, and you know my staff and I spoke to their president myself. He explained the whole concept to me. 'Someone who goes to get real footage from real people,' as he put it. Wait, Earth is still divided," he stammered. "Are you telling me another one of their presidents sent theirs?"

She suddenly looked tired. "No, Prime Minister. I'm saying that the position is not what we assumed. Looking back, I realized we made assumptions, taking the words of the president and his staff as the only things we needed to know. We assumed the human they sang praises of, James Arrington, was the only war correspondent on Earth, that it was a rare and prestigious job, and they were sending one to us in a gesture of allyship."

"What are you saying?"

"I'm saying that it is *just a job*. Dangerous, of course, hundreds have died over the years, but a job nonetheless. This is the first off-planet war they are covering, and they were professional and respectful about introducing the idea. But there's good reason they were shocked no other species has an equivalent. There isn't just one Earth war correspondent. Or two. There are *thousands*."

Yun stood in ankle-deep water outside the remnants of a home that had belonged to two male Holkanitan citizens, both mic'd. They had been lucky, visiting family on the day of the flooding, and both had survived. What they had returned to, when it was safe to do so, was no longer a home.

This interview was after an attack, comparatively safe considering the battles Yun had covered over the years. Since non-human war coverage was brand new, her schedule had been designed to give her and José a gradual learning curve. Dozens of reporters at Yun's HQ back on Earth were constantly gathering and explaining information about this conflict, putting it into context and studying like they hadn't since college.

Now, Yun spoke into the camera perched skillfully on José's shoulder, a camera that was rugged to the extreme, its innards easy to repair but also costing more than Yun would make in a year. "This is Yun Teng, Earth war correspondent, reporting from Rulkin City on the Holkanitan colony planet Balstona." Yun knew that back on her ship, her colleagues had already done three minutes of background introduction for viewers. They had the context; now it was time for her part.

"I'm standing with Ulti and Ramino, outside what used to be their home. Can you explain to the viewers what you told me?" Yun asked the man beside her, angling herself toward him.

Yun had surprised the couple when they realized she was fluent in Linkati, the most common language on their home planet and almost exclusively spoken in colonies. But while translators would suffice for Galactic viewers, when it came to those on the ground, human reporters knew there was no substitute for speaking the language. As soon as they'd passed the point of first contact and had the tech to teach them, many had started learning the basics of any languages they could pronounce.

By this point, Yun could passably speak two other alien languages. After studying the history of several conflicts, she'd prioritized which language she wanted to learn first, but knew she'd be continuing this component of her training for the rest of her career. Learning the past few hundred years of contextual history before going in for the coverage was one thing; learning the language was another, and learning a completely new body language was unprecedented.

Ulti gestured with his head in what Yun had learned was the equivalent of a nod. He hesitated for a moment, though, overwhelmed. She saw it in his eyes; their species shared that striking commonality. He spoke to her, meeting her gaze and ignoring the camera, as she'd instructed. "We… Ramino and I were visiting his sister. Her family lives over a hundred miles away. Suddenly our communicators started overwhelming us with messages from friends. We turned on the news and saw… The dam had been destroyed."

Ulti shifted his weight, his ears flicking back and forth in stress much like a horse. "I couldn't…understand, at first. I didn't know what I was looking at. I had to force myself to realize that I was looking at my town. It was just…gone. Razed to the ground by the water." Ramino intertwined his arm with his partner's and Ulti clutched his wrist in return. "We knew the military base nearby used it for power. But we didn't think the Inpelatonian would…"

"We lost everything we had," Ramino told her, taking over. His skin was paling, the equivalent of a human appearing on the verge of tears. "But we can only be grateful that weren't here. I can't count how many people I knew who were killed. How many children. Ulti and I will be in mourning for weeks."

Yun took the momentary pause to speak up with her next question. When José had given her the gesture that they were live, she'd felt that same feeling of clicking into place that she'd had hundreds of times before. From here on out, it was just a matter of doing her job. She'd already spoken to several other civilians and military personnel currently on the ground, ensuring they knew her job was not judgment. It was objectivity, to know their history and culture and ask the right questions to let the galaxy, including civilians on both sides of the conflict, learn more than they could before. To broadcast live, uncut, unaltered. To allow everyone watching to know the truth. Their truth.

The war is the war is the war.

Karen Avizur

The Psychologist

When you work as a psychologist, you see a variety of different people, and it's something the public by and large doesn't truly consider when they are introduced to one. Sometimes their first thought meeting me is, "Oh no, he's going to analyze and dissect my every move," and I'll admit that's instinctively true to an extent. The same way someone who works in the film industry experiences and analyzes a movie differently from anyone else.

But I've worked with a wide variety of patients since I've dedicated so much of my life to this career. I've seen those who suffer from the more common anxiety and depression that plagues so many of us these days. Also, those who suffer from more severe mental disorders like schizoaffective disorder or borderline personality disorder. And I've also treated people with the potential to become serious criminals, like pedophiles or those with antisocial personality disorder. Along with that, I'd published numerous papers and written a few books, even appeared on some talk shows.

Today was entirely different, though, and as far as I knew, unprecedented. I knew of the planet we'd recently discovered, the one with a 'primitive tribe' as they called it. Our media was swarmed with opinions on the way we'd been treating those who lived there, but everyone knew what happened when the Europeans arrived in North America. Everyone knew what would happen if aliens came to visit us first. But very few thought, or even cared, about what would happen if we first reached them. One man and his fans did, of course, and they called his care surrounding first contact, 'The Prime Directive'.

To our credit, there have been plenty of humans fighting for the rights of those on this new planet, and we've far from colonized it. To colonize a *whole* other planet was a venture that was far beyond our abilities, certainly far beyond our reproductive capabilities. Not to mention the terraforming it would take, resulting in genocide beyond anything we could imagine. But there had been an explosion of wonder and curiosity and we'd immediately started studying this intelligent species and the other animals and plants on their planet. Linguists and historians and scientists of all types, all fascinated by this unprecedented opportunity.

When I was picked up in a bland black sedan, at home to enjoy a Saturday off (short of any patient emergency calls) it wasn't as covert or frantic as I'd imagined it would be if I were in a movie. Badges were shown, revealing them to be with the Department of Homeland Security, and they explained that they needed my expertise as a psychologist. This had happened a few times before, but never someone sending a car to get me, much less with a government agent as the driver.

The building I was brought to was one among many in the warehouse district, though it had a much more severe atmosphere from the security that it boasted. It felt more likely that I was visiting a prison with the high fences topped with barbed wire, cameras everywhere I looked, armed guards, the works. But the demeanor of the guards was calm, not expecting trouble, it seemed. The man at the gate checked the badges against the faces of those who'd handed them over, scanning them with a computer in the booth in which he sat, and sent us on our way.

Considering how urgent it was for me to be brought to the facility, I was surprised then to wait at least half an hour in a stiff, uncomfortable chair in a bare-bones hallway outside an office. At one point someone came out with a rather thick packet of papers that amounted to a serious NDA for me to sign, but I'd expected nothing less, considering where I was. Someone eventually came to get me, a woman who stood like she would be more comfortable in uniform, and she held out her hand to greet me.

"Doctor Walton, I'm Lieutenant General Joann Wilder," she said, grasping my hand firmly as I stood and shook it. "Pleased to meet you."

"You as well. I'm still not sure why I'm here."

Wilder nodded once. "Your help is needed with several of the extraterrestrials that you've no doubt heard all about. We have several subjects here to study, a linguist translates for us, and we're having some trouble with them."

I blinked. Stared. "You…abducted them?" I finally asked.

Her eyebrows went up. "They volunteered. In exchange for technological advances for their people. Follow me, please."

Still feeling somewhat uneasy, I did so, the gears in my mind already churning rapidly, and I didn't give her a chance to explain any further; I directed the conversation first with a question. "How are they faring here?"

"They were all right," she replied. "But recently it's become problematic. They haven't asked to go back to their planet or anything, they know that's not an option, but they have expressed that they are homesick. It's just impossible for us to do anything for that, really."

"Impossible- You took them from their *planet*," I stated. "You didn't even plan for homesickness?"

"Of course we did," she scoffed, swiping a key card at a door we reached. A *beep* sounded and it unlocked, and she opened and held it for me. "The food we grow for them is naturally in keeping with their diet, they have materials for the same kind of games, and there are two of them so they can bond and share stories from back home."

"Two," I echoed.

"Yes, a male and a female."

Two. "That's…" I fell silent for a long moment as we walked down a cavernous hallway. "What exactly is it you want me to do here?" I asked, out of curiosity more than anything else.

"Speak with them through the translator," she answered. "I know their body language is much different than ours so I'm hoping speech will be enough for you to converse in a psychologically meaningful way. But they've been lethargic, not eating properly, reluctant to participate in scientific testing, and they won't tell us why."

"Why?" I echoed. We went through another door with another swipe of the woman's keycard and entered a brightly lit lab of some kind. The room was huge, leaving me feeling as if I'd stepped out of an office and into a stadium. "It seems staggeringly obvious as to-"

My voice caught in my throat as I laid my eyes on them.

They were in another, airtight section of the lab, for the obvious reason of needing different air to breathe. My first approximation of them when I'd seen a photo was that they were a lazy Lovecraftian god's version of a human, though of course that's probably specist. They were shorter, stouter, and reminded me of octopuses. Though they had two feet and two arms, they had three toes, larger feet, and three fingers. They were dark purple, colored to camouflage against a similar world of largely purple plants, we'd learned early on. They were covered in clothing that seemed similar to the tunics of ancient Rome.

They were incredible. I was stunned into silence in their presence.

The confines in which they lived were impressive, overall, and seemed to closely emulate their life back on their home planet. The area was huge, including a staggeringly high ceiling, had a dirt floor, and was populated by plants completely unfamiliar to me. It reminded me of an area that would be set aside for primates in a zoo, complete with a hut to the left of the enclosure that I figured served as their home.

The lieutenant general let me stare for a long moment before she spoke up, jolting me out of my reverie. "Our translator, Oscar, will help you," she told me, motioning to a middle-aged man who gave me a small wave as he walked over from what I was starting to think of as a 'display'.

"Oscar Hill," he said, shaking my hand.

"Doctor Earl Walton," I answered. "You can call me Earl. I just…" Wandering over to the glass wall, I noticed there was a section that had what I was guessing was a microphone built into it, with two chairs in front of it. I rubbed my hands over my face, taking it all in, and then dropping my hands to my sides as I let out a long breath. "Okay… Okay."

"I'll translate back and forth," Oscar told me. "They already knew you were coming." I nodded, taking a seat as Oscar did so as well. "Honestly I'm just grateful we have spoken language in common, considering how much trickier this would be if body language was an imperative function, like cats and dogs."

"They're-" I cut myself off, chewing on my lower lip as the two aliens walked over and stood near the microphone. I tried my best to guess as to their state of mind, their body language, to read their gaze, but their eyes were simply pools of turquoise blue and I lacked any reference point to gauge their state of mind from what I was looking at. "Okay. Ah…please tell them that I'm pleased to meet them. It's an honor to have the privilege, truly."

Oscar nodded and pressed the button on the microphone. The closest approximation I could find in my mind to the language he spoke was Xhosa, which is a beautiful language if you're unfamiliar with it. They replied. "They say it's very nice to meet you as well. They were told you were a doctor of the mind and here to help them."

"I am. I-I mean, I hope so." I paused. "What are their names?"

"The female, on the right, we call Jane, and the male is John."

I glanced at him. "*Their* names."

"Ah…" He pronounced them as best as he could, slowly, for me and we tried several times before I was able to echo them back to him.

"H'l'kah and H'con'set," I finally spoke.

Oscar nodded. "You got it."

I repeated the names in my mind multiple times. "Can you ask them what their life here is like?"

"This is it, basically," he told me. "Everything you see in-"

"Oscar," I said, meeting his gaze. "This is only going to work if I get to do my job, all right?"

He blinked and pursed his lips, nodding, and translated my question. He translated as they spoke back, and they paused to ensure he could keep up. "*Our day is repetitive,*" H'con'set told Oscar, though he focused his eyes on me. "*We wake when the orange light tells us it is day…and we have breakfast from the plants that grow here… We talk much of home… H'l'kah and I both enjoy creating things from wood… We used to make toys for the children back home… We have snacks, and then later we have dinner…*"

"*Much of the time is spent helping the scientists understand us… To know our world and to know our species… They also study many of the animals and plants back home… It is an honor to teach your kind of our kind.*"

I nodded slowly. "And what else do you do through your day in your free time?"

"*…We explore our dwelling and care for the plants… And we play games with pebbles, as we did back home.*"

"How do you feel about being here?"

"*…As I said, it is an honor,*" H'con'set answered.

"Yes, but beyond that. I was told you seem depressed. Do you feel depressed?"

"*…Yes. We miss home… But they take care of us here… Even the medicine is better than what we had…but I know the* *others back home have the same medicine now… As you know, your technology is greater than ours.*"

I paused, my mind trying to work in a way it never had before. What the hell was I doing? How was I supposed to make progress on a therapeutic level in this kind of environment? It was clear what the problem was, at least to me. Put two humans in a cage for months on end and no matter how giant and pretty the cage, no matter how Earth-like it is, no matter how similar the house was to a typical home, we would suffer. It was nothing more than a zoo, and they were our captives.

"In order to best help you," I said slowly, "I need to know how and what you think…and I need you to be honest with me, even if it is uncomfortable… Have you ever considered hurting yourself?"

Oscar glanced at me worriedly before he obediently translated the message.

The two aliens looked to each other and the female moved closer to the male. "*…I do not want to disturb the scientists' studies of us,*" H'con'set said. "*But I've done damage to myself and so has H'l'kah … Temporary damage that does not leave a mark…*" I heard Oscar swallow hard, but I didn't take my eyes off of H'con'set.

"Do you wish to die?" I asked.

"*…No, but also yes… I don't know why. We are unhappy here, and we've been here a short amount of time… We do not know how we will fare after years… And we know the work you do is important… And we promised this for the good of our people.*"

Something heavy churned in my stomach as I stared deep into the male's eyes. I've been at this job for most of my life, but never have I had such a disconnect between myself and a patient. There was nothing in his body language I could decipher as sadness or anger or depression. But there were words, and words were enough here.

"Thank you, H'con'set," I said, standing up. I bowed deeply, a custom I never used but regardless hoped would translate as submission and deep thanks. Looking both him and H'l'kah in the eyes, I then turned to Wilder, who was standing off to the side, looking uncomfortable and malcontent. "They need to go back home."

The woman stared at me, glancing behind me to Oscar and the two aliens and then back to me. "Wait, what?"

"You heard me."

"They are part of a billion-dollar study that-"

"Then replace them with others," I told her. My stance was stiff and barely veiled anger hid behind my gaze. "A month at a time, then send them back home and exchange them for others."

"Do you have any idea of the cost of-"

"I do not know the cost and I do not *care*," I snapped. "Let me put this in terms you can understand, because clearly even after overhearing that conversation I just had, you don't get it. You drop a bomb on a terrorist stronghold in Afghanistan where you think the leader of ISIS is hiding, and it turns out to be a preschool. And the news leaks. What happens?"

Wilder glared at me severely. "This is a far cry from something like that."

"They will die." Her eyes narrowed at me. "They will continue to self-harm, it will get worse, and they will either commit suicide or develop an eating disorder that destroys their health. They will die, and you'll have to find the *funds* to replace them anyway. And then? It'll happen again."

"That is why you're here," Wilder snapped. "This was not meant to be a five-minute chat that ends in you telling me how to do my job. It's meant to be the first of hour-long sessions just like any other patient of yours."

"That wasn't a chat; that was an evaluation of the patients, and it was so obvious that it only took five minutes. This isn't your job," I told her. "It's mine. I've been doing this for almost forty years and I'm telling you…you are killing them. In every way that matters. Zoos have the same problem, and they solve it with enrichment. But let me ask you, if it were two humans, two…ancient Sumerians taken by another species, what would you recommend as 'enrichment'? What could satisfy their minds, their *souls*, that would be sufficient?

"Because these are not snakes or koalas or even gorillas, to whom we've literally taught sign language. These are intelligent beings with the capacity to reach the same benchmarks as humans over the next ten thousand years on their planet, especially with our help. They can flourish, they can be magnificent, and we can have the privilege of watching that happen. But this is not the way. Another month, another two, they'll continue to get worse, regardless of any talk therapy I do with them weekly, even daily. They need their *home*. Their people."

"What do you expect me to report back to my superiors?" Wilder asked quietly, her expression terse.

"I expect you to report back…that this is unsustainable," I answered. "I can't control what the government does, I'm not foolish enough to think something like that. But the public at large can. Word will get out of how the captives are faring, it always does, and it's best to prevent the fallout from this entirely, don't you think?"

"We don't have the funding to do monthly transports for new candidates," she told me, something tired in her tone. "We just don't."

"Then don't." I held her gaze. "Do a month every two months, or every three, or four. Gather as much information as you can and then spend the rest of the time examining and evaluating that data. You could even take the same subjects over and over, as long as they get months at a time back home." I paused. "You brought me here for a reason. You knew they needed help. And this is what I'm saying you need to do to help them."

"You won't try talk therapy?" Wilder asked tightly.

My face fell. "No. Because that's not what they need. I won't treat a patient with something I know won't work." I hesitated, glancing back over my shoulder at them before looking back to the woman in front of me. "I did my job. Now it's up to you and your superiors. Ball is in your court. What comes next?"

Wilder looked over to the two aliens, stared at them for a long moment, and then said, "Next…I suppose I need to speak with the president about the well-being of our guests."

Karen Avizur

They're the Same

The first time I actually pet a dog, I was embarrassed, because despite the fact that a human was walking it on a leash, my first question was to confirm with the owner that it was a dog. All the vids I'd seen on Galnet had been of dogs that were large and terrifying and barking, or large and obedient and adorable, depending on the agenda of the one who'd posted the video.

"He's a breed called a basset hound," the human man told me. "They're renowned for their sense of smell and famous for being great trackers. I just love his ginormous ears."

The dog's ears were *comically* large. And the human said he hadn't known why the ears were that long, just that he loved them, but so many people from other species had asked that he finally looked it up. Apparently, it was extra help for sniffing things out, wafting the scents toward the dog's nose.

He also told me that the first time someone asked him if Max was a dog, he'd replied, "Either that or he's a raccoon but lied on his resume." But no other species understood that it was meant to be funny, so he told me now he just saves that joke for humans.

The dog was also nine years old, I was told, and the owner noted the gray hairs that illustrated that fact. Being much less intimidating than many of the dogs I'd seen in Galnet videos, I got past my fears and pet it, and its tail started wagging. Oh, and of course the talented sniffer sniffed me, and its nose was wet! That was a surprise. The human laughed and reassured me, saying that was normal.

My neighbor Eleanor had a breed that was common among off-worlders, a golden retriever by the name of Daisy. Eleanor had three young children and they all loved the dog. To see the little ones play with and pat the dog, watching Daisy wag her tail as she licked their faces (which they call *kisses*) and make them squeal about dog slobber, helped me be brave enough to ignore her giant teeth and claws and pat her as well. I learned the body language of their species quickly, and she's so happy to see me every time she spots me, that now I can't resist stopping to pat Daisy if I pass them on a walk.

Daisy is exceptionally well trained, to me at least, so when she acted out of sorts one evening when I had stopped to talk to Eleanor, I took note and backed up. "What's wrong?" I asked worriedly. Daisy was moving back and forth, staring at the forest, barking. She was pulling at her leash, then stopped, looking to the forest and then to Eleanor, continuing to bark. I'd never seen her like this.

"I'm not sure," Eleanor spoke, but didn't hesitate before crossing the empty street. I followed, curious. "She hears something or smells something that's worrying her." I was surprised to see Eleanor pull out her pulse gun from her purse, but realized she was going to walk into the neighboring forest. It wasn't horribly dangerous, we did live nearby after all, but there were predators that lived in it. My assumption was that if Daisy was concerned, that might be because there was one very close to where we were.

As for why we were, in that case, headed *toward* the forest instead of away, Eleanor told me, "It's not just that I think she smelled a predator. She's seen hallika twice at night through a window and barked as a warning for it to stay away. This is different. I'm worried."

Hallika were, I'd been told, bear-birds. After looking up photos of both Earth animals, I found it surprisingly accurate as a combination. If one of them was nearby and came too close to our village, they would allegedly run off if hit with a level 3 pulse. That didn't mean I wanted to test that theory, but I wasn't going to leave Eleanor and Daisy to pursue possible danger on their own. Even Daisy would be no match for one of these things if it attacked.

There was no path, so we just made our way as best we could through the forest led by a concerned and upset dog, glad the sun hadn't yet set. I eventually heard faint squealing and shrieking, the fur along my arms and back prickling in fear. "What is that?" I asked. "It sounds like something in pain."

The human didn't answer, but instead hurried her pace, and the brush cleared as we closed in on a horrific sight. It was indeed a hallika; it had attacked two grasslin, and there was blood everywhere. One was in its mouth, broken and dead, glassy eyes staring at nothing. My breathing sped up and I started to tremble. I couldn't help cursing repeatedly, but kept them at whispers, my instincts telling me to stay quiet.

But my curses were thoroughly drowned out by Daisy's ferocious barking, no longer pulling at the leash, instead standing in a way that was both intimidating and seemed ready to charge. To my surprise, the hallika let out a rumbly growl, but took several steps in the opposite direction. Daisy took a few steps forward, continuing her barking frenzy, and the hallika fled, one grasslin still in its mouth.

"Oh no," Eleanor lamented. I followed her gaze and my fur settled, my panic response slowly abating and my stance drooping, as I saw three extremely young grasslin next to a bush. The babies were too young to know what had happened, only that the sounds were of panic and death, which had caused them to huddle together.

"The parents were protecting them," I muttered in comprehension.

The forest was wild land, and there were carnivores that lived here; I'd known that. Death happened here every day, even to young offspring, and without us the hallika likely would have devoured the whole family. But it was strikingly sad to realize their parents were gone, to know that they needed help or they would perish to slow starvation.

Glancing at Daisy, I was surprised to see her body language had clearly and rapidly changed. She was now whimpering, and as Eleanor took a few small, slow steps forward, I took in a sharp breath as she dropped Daisy's leash. The dog went over to the grasslin, who were squealing in concern and fear, and immediately started licking them with her long pink tongue, continuing to whimper softly.

Eleanor knelt down on one knee, looking over the babies with her keen eyes, and I asked, "Why is Daisy doing that?"

"The same reason I'll call wildlife rescue," Eleanor answered softly, glancing up to me as she took out her communicator. "They're babies. And they're furry and squeaky enough for Daisy to know they need protection. She didn't lead us here because she heard the hallika. She came because she heard them."

As Eleanor made the call, I watched in awe as the animal that had descended from carnivores, the dog I'd seen get so excited over a beef-flavored bone that she'd practically been vibrating, fuss over the grasslin as if they were her own pups. Every once in a while, Daisy would glance to the dead parent that had been left behind and then look back at the offspring. After a minute or so, they seemed to settle, and Daisy laid down, curling around them protectively.

I couldn't take my eyes off the sight. Months and months of getting to know Daisy and seeing a few other dogs owned by humans in our village, and I'd never seen anything like this. But to Eleanor, it seemed to completely make sense. Something clicked with me in that moment. The pack bonding humans discussed, even joked about, this was part of what they meant. Simply hearing children of any species in distress, a human would rush to their aid, sometimes even if it was dangerous. All other sapient species had learned that.

But to see a dog do the same, to run towards the sounds of danger and then start grooming these babies as if they were hers… This was something I'd never heard discussed by the humans, and strangely enough, I realized it was because they considered it a matter of course. This was why they not only loved, but *bonded* with dogs. They were the same.

Humans had explained to me that they not only trusted their pet dog around their children, but felt comforted and protected with them around. I hadn't truly comprehended it until now. The dogs became family, and now I knew how. I'd seen Daisy's concern from afar and then her fearless confrontation of a predator to protect baby grasslin, and it was exactly what a human would have done.

Travel Class Ship

Back on Earth, before we had the tech to scour every inch of the ocean floor, humans used to dedicate their lives to finding old shipwrecks. Hoping to strike it rich, or at least fund their next mission. Nothing much has changed in that respect centuries later, except now the wrecks of ships are floating in open space instead of turning into a habitat on the ocean floor. And there are many more of them, when you put together every species in the galaxy.

Our company is called Geisler Retrieval, named after my partner David Geisler, even though the company is mine on paper. My last name was used for the ship, the Bellemare. David and Gemma technically work for me, though considering we're three long-time friends going from junker to junker for scraps, we're more like partners. After doing a gig like this for years, either you grow as close as siblings, or someone ends up stabbed with a screwdriver. And nobody's been stabbed yet.

We'd met while working together for four years at a ship repair space station, and so each of us were well-rounded in the ins and outs of our own little space boat. But officially, David was the mechanic, I was the pilot, and Gemma was the engineer. In a business, everyone plays to their strengths.

I heard the clanging of David's boots on the stairs. He stopped next to me, his hands against the low ceiling, looking at the screen in front of my console that imitated a wide window. "How're we looking?"

"Five by five. Was just about to call for you guys," I replied. Motioning to the other side of the console, I leaned back in my chair. "Just got within range. What's it look like?"

The ship we'd pinged as closest to us for our next scope was about a klick straight ahead, visible as a vague outline. I'd done enough of these to recognize it as Niltonian-made. The squids made good hardware, but the ships weren't quite up to the standards of ours. That's not to say they didn't fly well, but ask a pilot what they want, and Niltonian ships won't be a top-three choice.

"We have got…" David started, tapping at the console, and then making a motion that I recognized as zooming in. "Computer says HW-4318…tra-travel class," he managed to finish. He looked to me, and I met his gaze with a purse of my lips.

Travel class was tech talk for something that was, or doubled as, a home. It wasn't too surprising; we were only a few light years from a highway. But usually much of what we found was just derelict. A courier corvette that blew its engine, making it all but worthless to the company. A hauler that was past its prime and not worth pulling back to the station for repairs once they'd gotten the merchandise off. But of course, sometimes regular people had ship trouble, or even piracy.

So, these ships were fair game to board and clean out if left out in the void. But with travel class, unless you had the luck of finding one that had been abandoned on purpose because of cost of repair, and the occupants had been picked up by someone nearby, you ran a high risk of bodies. Sure, once you put them in cryo, the nearest embassy would accept them with a small token of their appreciation. It was just the matter of whether you wanted to deal with bodies. That's not why someone gets into this gig. If you wanted to do that, you'd work as crime scene cleanup.

Letting out a breath, I glanced at the screen, which showed us now at about half a klick away. At a quarter klick, the ship came to a stop, and I spoke without looking at David. "What do we have?"

Translation: We're boarding it.

With wordless acceptance of my decision, he tapped away at the screen before pausing to give me a summary. "Dead in the void," he said tightly. "No heat sigs. No beacon. We've got…four minor power sources still ticking." Those could be anything from lanterns to emergency equipment to a laptop. After at least a few months, as it seemed the case was here, anything on the ship had settled at 2.7 Kelvin, but almost all tech could survive that as long as it was turned off.

"Are we there yet, Lee?" Gemma asked, walking in and leaning against the wall.

"Yeah," I replied, not responding with banter, which probably confused her until I added, "Travel class."

"Oh."

"How's she look?" I asked, leaning forward to prop my elbows on my knees.

David shook his head, stone-faced. "Main entry was blown open." I let out a long breath. "No telling what's sealed off or what they took."

I nodded. "I know that. What don't I know?"

"Ah…standard is NIL992 engine, Brenner FTL Grade 2, Crafter console. That version will depend on when they bought it. This boat's been on the market for over a decade. Three rooms and…decent cargo area. Here you go." With a swipe, he threw the image he'd pulled up onto my screen.

It was a schematic, and we each looked it over for a good two minutes, committing it to memory. We'd bring a tablet for reference if we needed it, but it was always best to know the lay of the land ahead of time. "All right," I said, sitting up and turning my chair back to the console. "Suit up. I'll dock us at the main entry."

David nodded once in my peripheral vision as he and Gemma left me to my work.

Ten minutes later, I was pulling on my excursion suit. Our suits didn't need to be military grade in terms of line of sight or durability, but they were the one thing between us and a quick death. We didn't skimp, and we were good in these for thirty-two hours, much more than we'd ever needed. After a thorough double-check of each of our suits by the other two of us, we went into the airlock, sealing the door behind ourselves. Then we decompressed, I turned off artificial gravity, and I hit the button for the exit.

I'd secured us over the entry, ours was bigger than theirs by about half, but there was no airtight seal for a transfer like this. Our ship had just done the easy thing and clamped on, drilling stabilizers into the inside walls, since it was rarely worth the hassle of being airtight. We never left our suits. Floating inside, I looked around.

Entry was standard and I saw what I expected: the airlock door inside had also been blown, charred metal and a hole where the latch used to be. The void sometimes sucked things out, so if anything else had been in there, it was long gone. The first stop was the cockpit and David led the way. Like virtually all ships, even if they were carpeted over it, this one had metal flooring that our boots held to magnetically so we could walk.

The door was already wide open once we got there, so David went in and headed straight to the console. Attempting to boot it up, if there was dormant power, would've killed it instantly because of the temperature. So, this part was all hands and sight. David ducked under the console with a screwdriver, doing a backwards limbo in the weightlessness, his mag-boots keeping him oriented. My breathing was the only thing I heard, the clank of his boots soundless in the void.

A minute or so passed before he came back out with the motherboard. He handed it to me. *"Good condition,"* he signed. *"Ship must've powered down before the doors blew. It didn't fry."*

That was surprising, but good news. The motherboard tended to be the second-most valuable thing on a ship like this, the first being the FTL drives. Those, we'd save for last, though. They were the heftiest, and we'd fill our packs with anything and everything else first.

Gemma had the power gauge in-hand and circled the room with it. She found a personal heat box, usually for meal storage. She glanced inside, only to see that it was empty, and motioned to us that it was one of the power sources we'd been looking for. Going back down the hall, she led the way this time, going into the kitchen/living/dining area that opened up on our left.

Scanning the room with only my eyes, it looked pretty typical. The blast of the entry opening had splayed open most of the cabinet doors, revealing typical supplies. David checked the fridge, which was still shut since it had a latch (a surprising number of people stored valuables there) and I checked the inside of appliances. The oven and microwave were both empty, aside from a few pans stored in the oven that were floating in zero-g.

Turning to David, who'd walked over to me, he shook his head, and we both looked to Gemma. She found a coffee maker and gave us the signal again. Then we continued down the hall. All the doors were shut.

Pulling the manual latch and opening the door to the first room on the right, it was some sort of office. Gemma headed in and found a laptop floating in the back corner of the room. Picking it out of the air, she signed to us *power* one more time, then tucked it away in her backpack. We spent the next ten minutes or so sifting through the detritus floating around in the air, grabbing hold of anything that looked sharp as we went. It was almost impossible for a letter opener to pierce our suits, but it paid to be paranoid.

Gemma gestured to her bag, in which was the laptop, power source three. "*If this was pirates, why leave the electronics?*" she asked.

"*Cargo was worth more?*" David suggested. That was likely. He said they had decent cargo storage, so it could be they ran a small business. We'd check cargo, but if that had been their target, it meant everything there was long gone.

The next door, on the left, was a bedroom. As far as I could tell, nothing violent had happened here. The mattress was still held to the bed, standard procedure, but various untethered objects littered the space around the room. None of them were valuable, but we found a jewelry box in a drawer that had quite a few trinkets in it. Whether they were worth anything was yet to be determined, but it went in my bag.

The fact that the jewelry was there made the pit in my stomach heavier. And the fact that we'd be selling it made me borderline queasy. It was all legal, the owners were gone and the hassle of finding the owner's next of kin somewhere in the galaxy was a waste of time for what was largely a box of knick-knacks, but it didn't make jobs like this any easier. I preferred abandoned long-haulers where we'd pluck power storage clips out of their cases one by one.

David pulled the entry latch to open the last door on the left. Nothing happened.

Looking to both of us, meeting our gazes in turn, all of us were tense. Someone had locked this from the inside.

"We're still short one power source. It could be in engineering," Gemma signed. That was unlikely. Gear wasn't stored there. No one even went in there unless something needed fixing or for maintenance.

I hesitated, then nodded to my right. Going down the hallway, we opened the door to the back of the ship. Our boots hit corrugated metal soundlessly as we went down to engineering. Gemma did a sweep and David examined the drives. He gave me a thumbs up after a thorough examination, which meant nothing was visibly damaged. We'd need to test each individually once we got them back to the ship, though. Eventually Gemma shook her head, not having found anything.

Our next stop was cargo, and after opening the door, no one went in. Nets and straps for tying things down hung lazily in the air. Shelves lined the walls. Aside from that, it was empty. What we hadn't been able to see from aboard the Bellemare, since it had been on the opposite side, was that the cargo bay door had been breached. After the valuable goods had been taken, it had been left to the vacuum once they unsealed and detached. I shut the door.

Going reluctantly back to the one door we hadn't opened, I stopped in front of it and met David's gaze, tilting my head in its direction. He nodded, pulling out the handheld laser cutter from his pocket and taking it to the latch. Skillfully cutting away the outer layer, he continued through and disabled the lock. Finally, he pulled the latch and slid the door open.

All of us shut our eyes. I only knew that because I knew my crew, and my eyes had immediately closed. As soon as we'd seen what was in the room, instinct kicked in to cut off line of sight.

Taking in a slow breath of slightly stale, cool air from my suit, I reopened my eyes. Two Niltonians were sitting on the floor in the far corner, tentacles wrapped around each other. A male and a female, from the coloring. They were stuck in place, I knew, having fused to the metal behind them when it cooled. That meant the gravity hadn't gone out until later. That meant we didn't even know how long they'd sat there, the void creeping in through the walls until it claimed every heat source available.

And then I was moving. Because this was a child's room, and floating in the air near them was the last power source: a small cryopod.

As fast as I could go without accidentally launching myself off the ground, I went over to it and pulled it down the floor. Leaning over it, I took in a sharp breath. A Niltonian child lay inside. My gaze darting to the control screen, I realized David and

Gemma were crouching at my side, on each end of the pod, holding it in place.

"*We've got to get it back,*" I signed to them before pulling the pod into the air.

"*Do you think she's alive?*" Gemma asked, meeting my gaze with tears in her eyes.

"*She?*"

Gemma motioned. "*Top of her head. Blue's turning purple.*"

"*There's no way to tell her condition. I can't activate the computer in this temperature, not even high-end gear like this. And if she is, we want to check in the medbay, just in case.*"

Gemma took a breath and nodded as I looped my arm under the pod and carried it out to the hall. With her in the lead and David steadying the pod from behind as I guided it through the air, Gemma suddenly stopped and turned around, holding up a finger. She went back into the room and a few moments later came out with a stuffed animal that looked worn out from love. I gave her a soft smile as our eyes met briefly and then we continued on.

Once we'd transferred back over, back in the pressurized ship with 1g under our feet, we then left our packs in the hall beside our helmets. Not bothering to take the time to change, David and I both took a handle at each end of the pod to carry it. Gemma led the way into our med bay. It was modest, as these things go, but while it might not be top of the line, it had everything we needed.

Placing the pod on the gurney, I finally held down the power button and when the screen lit up, I let out a harsh breath I hadn't noticed I was holding. Running a hand down my face, I then selected menu options to go into the metadata.

"How long?" David asked, knowing what I would look for first.

I paused as I selected menu options to get where I wanted to go. "Galactic time…2.6 cycles," I whispered. That was about 1.9 years on Earth.

"Oh, frap," Gemma muttered.

"Everything…everything's fine," I managed to say in grateful astonishment, after navigating over to the menu that monitored the process. "She should be fine."

Silence fell as we all considered everything we knew, and everything we didn't know.

"Could she be hurt?" Gemma asked.

Pausing and biting my lip, I shook my head. "I don't know. But I don't think so. Her parents…" My voice faded.

"They ran to her," David muttered. "Maybe they were given the option to be boarded willingly, maybe not. Either way, they do what's instinctive. Run. Hide. Lock the door behind them. Main entry is forced, the ship opens to vacuum. The girl's emergency cryopod is in her room for easy access, of course, but theirs…" He let out a long breath and slumped against the wall.

"They wouldn't risk opening the door," I said, crossing my arms across my chest tightly. "So, they made sure she was safe." We all stared at the pod for a long moment.

"We get her to the embassy first, right?" David asked, looking to me. "They'll open the pod and find next of kin."

"What if there is none?" I asked tiredly. "Two parents running a business that needs to take the highways, and they run it from their home with their kid. If you've got anyone on-planet, chances are slim that this is how you live your life. And how do we make sure she doesn't fall through the cracks? If they cut power to the ship before they took the cargo, and this damn boat really is flyable, it could be everything she has."

The rules of the game when it came to our job were straightforward. Any abandoned vessel was fair game for scavenging, but if you wanted the ship, there were hoops to jump through. Next of kin to search for, paperwork to fill out, maybe a lease that still wasn't paid off. *Probably* a lease that wasn't paid off, if you're being honest with yourself. That was a bigger fish for a bigger company to handle.

But nothing we'd seen had looked fried. We could put the motherboard back, tow it into the nearest space station, and invest to fix the parts that had been blasted away when they'd been boarded and robbed. The Niltonian girl might want to sell it. She might want to keep it. Whatever she wanted, though, I felt compelled to be the one to look her in the eyes and ask her, and then to make sure it happened. If we got her and the ship back to Niltonian territory and put in some ridiculous claim, we'd wrap ourselves up in this situation and make sure she didn't get screwed over if there was a company holding the lease.

Of course, that meant being the ones that told her that her parents were dead.

"What's the play?" Gemma asked softly.

Clasping my hands together, I pressed my knuckles to my lips. Seconds ticked by. My crewmates were silent. The faint sounds of various appliances in the room hummed, and that was it. Finally, I lowered my hands and stepped up to the pod, tapped at the screen, and selected the command to open. Then I pulled over a stool and sat on the edge, waiting anxiously.

The process took a few minutes that stretched, and I felt each second tick by like it was pulled through molasses. Eventually, the lid unlatched with a *snick* and opened gradually to a wide angle, revealing her. I took one of her tentacles in my hand, which was still chilly even though her blood was pumping again, hoping that having something to hold onto would help her steady herself. I'd come out of cryo before, and it wasn't totally pleasant.

Her eyelids twitched and slowly opened as she breathed shallowly.

"Hi," I said softly. "You're coming out of cryo. You're safe. Do you understand me?"

A moment paused before she made a small sound that my chip rendered as untranslatable. But her tentacle squeezed my hand.

"Take your time. Focus on your breathing."

After a few more breaths, the girl managed to let out a bubbly sound that translated as, "Hi."

As her two large black eyes opened and met my gaze, I blinked back tears. Then I took a deep breath and asked her for her name.

***

Special thanks to /u/GiantEnemyCrabThing on Reddit for proofing the science on this one!

Karen Avizur

Unavailable

My favorite thing ever is visiting a new planet. At least, it used to be. It's not anymore because when we get there, I don't even get to get off this stupid ship. Being on the run is a lot more exciting in movies, for sure.

Mom's job as an interplanetary chef, helping humans and aliens talk about culture and stuff, was the best, because we don't just meet aliens, we meet *famous* aliens. All my friends back on Earth are lucky to even see one in real life, and over the past two years, I've met loads. I can tell my friends how squidgy a Nilltonian's tentacle is when you shake appendages, how smelly Garkula are, and that you never want to touch a Yuluti because they're slimier than a frog. Not to mention I've gotten to eat a bunch of different alien foods. Some are so, so good.

My younger brother and I are homeschooled, since we travel so much. I'm eight, but Aiden is only five, so there's really not much he can learn yet. He knows his numbers and letters in English and Spanish, and sometimes we play games to teach him about stuff from other planets, but that's it. He's real smart, though. I'm glad, because being an older brother is hard work, and if he was dumb, he would need so much help from me when he starts learning real math and science.

When Mom started her new job, she and Dad sat us down and explained how important it was that we listen to them when we're off the ship. I was only six, but I still remember how I felt during that conversation. It was exciting, and they made sure I knew it was going to be great (and Mom was going to make so much money!) but meeting aliens was like meeting people from other countries. They might be really different, and they might be nice, but they might also say mean things. They also might *do* mean things. It was like a level two stranger-danger talk.

The aliens understood we were only kids though, so when Aiden did something like poke the leg of a Yuluti ambassador and then start crying because his hand got all slimy, they didn't get too upset. Plus, of course, aliens had kids too, so sometimes they let us play together as they talked. Some of the kids were so tiny, some were big, some were cute, and…well, yeah, there was this one that was *so ugly*. But I didn't say anything mean at all. I just smiled. I waited until we got back to the ship to tell Mom and Dad how creepy that one baby was.

I thought this was Mom's job and it would always be the same. Then they killed Dad. And we've been trying to get back to Earth ever since.

Mom didn't tell me exactly what happened. Maybe she will when I'm older, but I think she figures the details don't matter. Why would I care whose president got angry at our president and decided to start some war? Everything was fine, and then someone was shooting at us at through the window of a restaurant. We rushed Dad back to the ship, but he died. The alien working as our planetary escort made sure we got off-planet, but she had to stay behind. Her name was Milu. She was nice. I haven't seen her since.

Once Mom jumped our ship into the middle of nowhere, time sort of stopped. Aiden hated being in the med room with Dad's body, so he just curled up in a ball under the covers in his bed and stayed there. It was different for me for some reason. For a while, I couldn't look away from his body. But eventually I left the room, left Mom clutching Dad's hand as she silently cried, and then I couldn't bring myself to go back in again. She put Dad in cryo and promised me and Aiden that when we got back to Earth, we'd have a proper funeral.

Later that night, Mom gave me another talk. Like, level three stranger-danger. She told me a lot of aliens would be looking for us. Not us in particular, but all humans. Once we got back to Earth, we'd be safe, but she was going to have to 'take the long way around', whatever that meant. There were some aliens that would help us, so we'd go to them along the way. She said that until we were back on Earth and safe, she had to turn off anything that connected us to the galaxy, so I couldn't even talk to my friends anymore.

"This isn't for forever, Calvin," she assured me. "It's just for a month or so, maybe less. Then we'll be back on Earth and everything will be okay."

It was hard to sleep that first night, and I had nightmares when I did. Aiden woke me in the middle of the night to sleep in my bed. That's fine, especially since he doesn't kick me in his sleep anymore. And to be honest, it was nice to have the company. To know he was right there.

The next few weeks were pretty boring, to be honest. Mom even made me keep doing my schoolwork, which didn't seem fair, but I think she needed something to do. Even grownups get bored, and she didn't have anyone else to talk to. She went a little crazy cleaning the ship and checking on the engine and stuff. She always called it our reliable old rust bucket, because we'd got it used, but *Apollo* (that's our ship's name) wasn't rusty. She was just old. All that was important was that she was reliable.

Our latest stop was on some planet we'd never been to so Mom could visit some alien she'd only met in person once. She landed in a place out of the way so we wouldn't be noticed, and her orders before she left were the same as always. We were not allowed to take even one step outside the ship. And if anyone pressed the doorbell, we weren't allowed to let them in no matter what they said over the intercom. Assume they're lying, she said. Mom tells me stories sometimes about how both humans and aliens lie and are tricky to get what they want.

So, when someone *did* ring the bell, I told Aiden to lock himself in our bedroom and I ran to the bridge to look at the screen that showed who was outside.

There were three of them, and they looked sort of like humans if we were lizardy and green and looked like we might explode from having too many muscles. I recognized the species as Ankili. One of them pressed the button again and my heart raced as I stared worriedly at the screen, wringing my hands. Then he held down the audio button to speak, looking at the tiny camera lens.

"Come on, humans, I know you're in there."

My breath hitched and I swallowed hard. I knew that was bad. All humans were hiding from everyone. If they knew we were here, that was really bad.

"It's not a big deal, we just need to speak with the captain," he continued. "Then we'll be on our way. My troop and I don't care as long as you're leaving soon, but we have to make sure you aren't here to cause trouble. I have the info on this ship. I know I'm looking for Captain Victoria Davis and her two sons, Aiden and Calvin."

I didn't move. No way to know if they were telling the truth, and they probably just wanted to kill us. I couldn't even guess at how they were feeling because faces were so different. It wasn't like one of them would say something evil and then turn to his buddy and wink.

How long has Mom been gone? The clock said it was 18:24, and Mom had told me if everything went according to plan, she should be back by 20:00. That was a pretty long time for us to stay in this standoff, and I doubted they would leave if I asked them politely.

"All right, fine. Have it your way." The one talking backed up with his buddies and pulled out a gun.

My eyes widened as he pointed it at the door, and he got off three shots before I leapt forward, held down the audio button and cried, "Wait! Stop!" before the force could break through the shielding layer.

The shooting stopped and they froze. I grimaced, backing up. *Great. What do I do now?*

The alien came back to the speaker and pressed the button again. "Who is that? Aiden? Calvin?"

"Oh no oh no oh no," I whispered, clenching and unclenching my fists.

"Come on now, talk to me."

No turning back now. I reluctantly stepped forward and held down the button again. "Yeah, this is Calvin. Just go away. We don't want any trouble." That's what characters always said in the movies, so I figured that was what I should go with. Then again, saying that usually resulted in the trouble they didn't want, so maybe I should've said something else.

"That's fine, Calvin. Can we talk to your mother?"

I hesitated before holding down the button to speak again. "No. She's busy. She said to tell you to go away."

"Calvin, this is important. Your mother needs to come talk to us." He paused. "Unless she's not there. Did she leave the ship?"

I pressed the button again to yell, "She's here, she's just *busy*. She's *taking a giant poop!*"

The alien leaned back and there was a long pause. "She's…using the toilet?"

"Yeah, she's been in there for ages and you're being really rude," I snapped. "How would you like it if someone kept banging on the door when your tummy hurt and you're farting and having diarrhea?"

There was a longer pause as the alien turned to his two buddies. I wondered what he was saying. Did they know about human poop? Did aliens even get tummy aches if they ate something bad? If they didn't, they might not believe me, but that makes no sense. No aliens could eat *everything*, right? Some stuff was extra and needed to be peed and pooed out.

"Calvin…can you tell your mother that it's illegal for your ship to be here and it's really important we talk to her?"

I pushed down hard, angrily, on the console speaker button once more. "You've just got to wait! I don't even want to go in there! I'll probably throw up if I have to again. It smells like a garbage dump had a baby with a sewer. When she gets food poisoning she's like a weapon of mass destruction. We don't even have any windows on this stupid ship and that dinky little fan isn't helping at all. I wouldn't be surprised if *Mom* threw up. And if she has to walk down here, she'll probably poop her pants and the whole ship is going to stink. *Are you trying to get my mom to poop her pants?*"

Letting go of the button, I stumbled back a couple steps, breathing hard. Blinking rapidly, I glanced at the closet to my left. There was a gun in there. I knew how to use it. Mom and Dad had taught me, in case of emergency. But there was no going back from that. If the aliens came in and saw me holding a gun in my hand, all bets were off. They'd kill me. I would do everything in my power to protect myself and Aiden, but I wasn't stupid enough to think I could kill all three like some action movie hero.

They talked amongst themselves for a surprising amount of time. It was probably only a minute or two, but it was something. It meant they were maybe trying to figure out if I was lying, or if I was telling the truth and was it really worth it to break down a door to an angry, pooping, probably armed human?

Finally, he pressed the button again. "Okay, uh…Calvin…tell her we'll wait, okay? But this ship isn't going anywhere. If you try to take off, we'll shoot you down."

Stunned into silence, I paused for a moment before pressing the button long enough to say, "Fine!" and then backed off. I stared at the screen, watching them. One stayed there and the other two went left and right. A few minutes later, they arrived back where they started and, I guess, talked about how long they thought humans can poop for. I finally sat down in the chair in front of the console, letting out a long, shaky breath.

It was only ten minutes later, all three of them still waiting and occasionally saying things I couldn't hear, that there was suddenly movement. They each leapt in different directions, and I caught sight of one of them taking his gun back out. I jumped to my feet and grabbed the console, leaning in close as if it would give me a better view outside. Seconds ticked by like hours and I bounced on my feet, desperate to know what was going on.

Then the distinctive *cluck* of the front door opening echoed down the hall. "Calvin? Aiden?" shouted my mother's voice.

"Mom!" Bolting out the door and down the hall, I turned and sprang into her arms, which wrapped tightly around me.

"Oh, thank goodness," she breathed in my ear, holding me close.

"Aiden's in his room. He's fine," I murmured.

She turned to press the button to shut the door and held me back at arm's length, holstering the gun that I just now noticed she'd been holding. I guess I knew what happened to the aliens. "How long were they here?" she asked. "What happened? I saw scorch marks on the door."

"Like…fifteen minutes," I told her. "They tried to talk me into letting them in."

"But they didn't force it? What did you tell them?"

I grinned. "I told them you were pooping. Want to know what I said?"

Vessel

My partner, Officer Brian Krause, and I were at a minor dispute between neighbors when we heard the screams from another apartment. We'd been called to the address for one of those cases where basically our job was to say, "Hey, calm down," or "Let them finish," over and over until things were settled. Then suddenly everyone involved was staring down the hallway with wide eyes and my partner and I bolted toward the sounds.

By the time we arrived, the worst of it was over. A woman, covered in blood spatter, knelt over her victim, having stabbed him multiple times in the stomach. He was still alive, pupils dilated in panic and gaping like a fish out of water, but wasn't long for this world. Even if medics materialized in that instant, the damage was too severe.

In the woman's hand was a chef's knife, and she dropped it when we came in, guns in hand. "I had to!" she screamed, scrambling backwards along the floor, leaving bloody handprints as she went. "I had to, the voices, they made me!"

"Damn it," growled my partner, dropping to the man's side as I rushed over to the woman. "You got her, Stevens?"

"I got her." Yanking the woman to her feet, I pulled out the cuffs and put them swiftly on her wrists as she sobbed, and my partner called it in.

"Release her, or you shall become our new vessel," echoed a voice in my head.

I froze in shock and felt the woman grow still in my grip. "Did you hear him too?" she whispered.

The male voice was almost mechanical, like something I'd expect to come out of Apple's latest virtual assistant. "What the hell is this?" I muttered, looking to the woman and then around the room, puzzled.

"I repeat, release her immediately."

"Krause, did you hear that?" I asked without looking to my partner.

"Hear what?"

"Please, ma'am, please help me," the woman whimpered. "They made me do this." Exhaustion blanketed her tone and made me even warier, a finger of ice tracing its way down my spine.

"He's gone," Krause said tightly, drawing my gaze. I swallowed hard, looking at the eyes of the deceased, staring up at the ceiling. "Hey, bring her down to the squad car and I'll secure the scene," he told me. His eyes narrowed worriedly at the expression on my face. Five years working together, you get to know your partner. "What is it?"

"Something…weird's going on," I said slowly. My eyes slid around the room as if I could spot the source of the voice. "I'm hearing… This is screwed up, but she said she was hearing a voice, and I-" A sharp dagger cut its way through my skull and I let out a shriek, my knees giving out, my hands going to my forehead as I shut my eyes against the pain.

"Stevens!" my partner barked. I heard him dart to my side. "What is it? What's wrong?"

I rapidly blinked my eyes, looking around, tense against the fear of the pain. "I don't…"

He stared at me worriedly, as if I might keel over at any moment. "Migraine?" I shook my head, my shoulders stiff as my eyes scanned the room once more. But who was I kidding? If Krause couldn't hear it, what made me think I was going to see it? "I'll get her down to the car," he told me, helping me to my feet.

"No," I said quickly. "No, I got it."

"You sure?"

Hell no. "Yeah." I took the woman by the arm, guiding her around the corpse and out into the hallway. Once we were out of earshot of my partner, as well as the neighbors who were peeking out of their apartments, I spoke up quietly. "What is this?"

"I don't know," she muttered. "It just hurt. It saw what I saw, heard what I heard. It wouldn't leave. I'm so sorry, I just had to kill him, it hurt so much, I was going insane." We started down the stairs back to the first floor. "I had to make it stop. The voices, they threatened me, my family. I had to. I had to kill him."

"Who was he?"

"I don't know."

We made it a few paces out into the foyer on the first floor before a female voice, just as stiff and formal, spoke in my head, stopping me dead in my tracks. "This is your last warning. Unhand the woman or you will become our next vessel."

"Vessel for what?" I snapped. Despite the fear churning in my stomach, I tried to project an angry, firm tone. At the same time, I was glad there wasn't anyone else around to see me talking to myself, because I was still half convinced I was losing my mind.

She didn't respond. I just received another bolt of lightning to my skull and crumpled to the ground under its weight. My grip on the woman's arm only tightened and she came with me with a cry. Gasping for air as I cradled my head in my other hand, my face twitched in anxiety, my eyes darting around, desperate for an enemy. Desperate for someone or something to lash out at, to point my gun at.

"It's gone," the woman choked out with a sob. "Oh, thank you, oh my god, they left…"

And I wish I could have said I didn't know what she meant, but I heard it. There was a buzz in my head, faint and tinny, feeling like a low bass echoing through my skull. Whatever they were, they had left her. And they had come to me. "Complete your job of the arrest," the male voice echoed in my head. "Then we'll have our first assignment for you."

"What the hell is that supposed to mean?" I barked, shoving myself to my feet and pulling the woman with me. "Who are you?" I received no answer and my upper lip curled in fury. "Who are they?" I snapped at the woman, turning her to face me.

"I don't know," she whispered, tears still slipping from her eyes.

With a lack of anything else to do, and feeling like I had eyes staring at me from every direction, I brought the woman out to the car and put her in the backseat. I called in the arrest and barely needed to wait a few minutes before backup showed up. A fresh corpse will do that.

Once she was transferred to another car to be brought back to the precinct for booking, I looked over to Krause who was talking to some of the crime scene techs before they went upstairs. They then nodded and headed inside, and he turned to me, walking over. "What the hell was that about, upstairs?"

"I might be losing it," I told him quietly.

"You are the one woman I can guarantee will never lose it," he shot back, "so what is it?"

"There's a voice in-"

The next stab of pain dropped me to my knees again, but Krause caught me before I hit the ground. "What the hell?" he cried. "Stevens, what is going on?"

It wouldn't let me talk about it. That wasn't difficult to piece together from the zaps I was getting, like a dog with a bark collar. "I don't...know what's going on," I said carefully as I steadied myself on my feet. "I might just..." Working my mouth thoughtfully, I met his gaze. "I think I got a song stuck in my head. Or something." The look he gave me was pure bemusement. "I don't know the name of it. From that movie, A Beautiful Mind. You seen it?"

His face slowly went slack. "Uh…yeah. Yeah, a few years back." He fell silent, waiting for me to continue the conversation. It took me a moment, but I at least knew what was inside my head was mine. They wouldn't have let me make that metaphor if they'd known what it meant. *It saw what I saw, heard what I heard…*

"Make up an excuse to leave," the voice ordered. "You need to find your next target. You know you have no choice."

"Understood," I answered. Krause stared, blank-faced, waiting to follow my lead. "Krause…I think those headaches I got are getting worse," I said. My tone was that of a bad actor, and I knew he'd see right through it, but just in case, I'd drop another hint. "I need to go home, so I need you to stay and take care of the crime scene." My gaze steadied. "Stay on my six."

Nodding slowly, he spared a glance back to the other squad cars that had arrived before meeting my gaze firmly. "Gotcha," he said.

With that, I got into our car, Krause's worried eyes following me, started the engine, and pulled back out onto the street. I didn't look back, just trusted that he'd follow me. I had no other choice.

Turning off my radio against calls from dispatch or any other officers, I let out a breath. "All right. We're alone. Why are you having people kill other people?"

"If it comforts you, they are not people," the male voice told me. "They are not of your planet. They hide among you, escaped convicts. Violent criminals."

Call me crazy, but I wasn't about to trust the voices in my head on something like that. But it wasn't as if I could call them on it. As far as I knew, Earth wasn't even close to this kind of technology, whatever this was. For all I knew, the CIA could have developed it and was targeting people, or some rogue black ops crap that belonged in a Hollywood movie. At this point, though, it didn't seem likely. I knew how humans operated, I knew our government and those of other countries, and there were way easier ways to kill people than this.

Though it did give them a patsy, I realized. That could tilt the scales to make it worthwhile. But if there were going to be multiple victims, we'd put it together. Especially if the voices were jumping from person to person, adding onto the witness list, the FBI would probably find the pattern without too much trouble. Bottom line was that it was messy and caused too much trouble. The only ones who wouldn't be worried about the fallout were ones who didn't have to deal with it.

Such as, for example, aliens who could take off when their murder spree was done.

What did I just get myself into?

I was still hoping I was crazy. Of course I was; it would be easier to deal with a mental break than something like whatever this was. But it was hard to deny the evidence of the past hour. I kept my eyes on the road, refusing to look in the rearview mirror for Krause. It was agonizing, feeling strikingly alone and trapped like a rat in a maze, but I somehow stopped my eyes from checking.

"Who's the target?" I asked. "Where am I going?"

"The address is 142 18th Avenue," the male voice told me. "Can you find your way there?"

"Yeah," I muttered. Driving in what I knew was the general direction, I waited until I hit a red light and I punched the address into my GPS. "I'm a law enforcement officer, you know," I told the voices. "You made a good choice with me. I can lie and say they were aggressive, possibly frame them for a crime, and then we can move onto your next target."

I wasn't sure whether they'd buy the bluff, since if they had a decent amount of information on humans, they'd know such a rapid change of attitude on the fact that I'd been recruited to be an assassin was unusual. But it was worth a shot.

"We've seen such cases in our studies," the voice replied. "Those who were caught, at least. But that's not our concern. These criminals need to be eliminated and the way in which we accomplish that isn't important."

"Why recruit humans, then? Why not come do the work yourselves?"

"The technology we use is beyond your comprehension," he said, the strange tone of his voice making the statement sound matter of fact rather than insulting. To be honest, I figured he was right. "You only need to understand that this is the most efficient way of carrying out our mission."

Mission. Were these soldiers? That could change things. I had been playing with a lot of hypotheticals, but what if this was some kind of precursor to an invasion? Or what if I was doing the dirty work for aliens who were in the process of invading, if the victims were people who had discovered the truth? That was a paranoid thought, but seemed like the right level of paranoia considering the situation.

That could go downhill quickly, though, if this was something bigger than me, bigger than my country even. If I was just a pawn in a game. I wasn't about to help some aliens take over the planet, that was for sure. But there was no out for me. The only advantage I had right now was that I was in contact with them, like a hostage taker inside a building. If they hung up the call, I had no connection and I'd just be on the outside worried about everything I wasn't seeing and didn't know.

We only had about ten minutes until we arrived at our destination though, so I knew I had to talk fast as well as stay smart. "Are there any other places on our planet where these criminals are hiding?" I asked. "Other countries? And how many are there?"

"Not your concern."

I pursed my lips. Not a surprising response. "It is my concern though, because this is my planet," I explained. "Just like you have your mission protecting your people from violent criminals like these, I protect mine. So, if this is a matter of ten people or a matter of ten thousand, it matters to me. I want to keep my planet safe."

There was a long pause. "There are only twelve, and they're all in your general vicinity. Three have been eliminated already, including the most recent one you witnessed."

Damn it. That meant there was definitely more than one puppet here. The woman I arrested for sure had only killed that man. I wondered what Krause was up to, if he had reached out to the precinct for backup, if he had any idea of how to stop what this was. Though, I was in the middle of it, and I had no idea what to do next.

I'd arrive at the address, make my way into the apartment with my gun, and then what?

"How come they look human?" I suddenly asked.

"It's a biological adaptation, so they could blend in. Even if they were satisfied with hiding, your air is not breathable to our native biology."

Our. That was a big word. So, these 'criminals' were one of his species, whatever they were. That could mean criminal, but it could also mean refugee. It could mean whatever the extraterrestrial equivalent of Witness Protection was. Of course, I wasn't going to kill anyone these voices told me to, but the possibility of them escaping some sort of oppressive regime by turning themselves into humans seemed rather drastic. Though, as the voice had so succinctly put it, the tech was beyond my measly human brain.

My phone rang in my pocket, and I narrowed my eyes, taking it out. The caller ID read *Krause*. "It's my partner."

"He believes you're ill. You can ignore his calls without cause for alarm. Turn the phone off."

"All right." Flicking the tab on the side to set it to vibrate, I looked back to the road and, without looking, swiped to answer the call, putting it face down on the seat next to me.

Taking a turn onto a main road, my wishes for a car crash to materialize and delay us still going unanswered, I chewed on my lower lip. "This is gonna sound strange, but this is probably the coolest thing to ever happen to me," I said. "You know humans haven't contacted any alien civilizations. We don't even know you exist. I mean, do we?"

"There has been sporadic contact, but none with your authorities."

"Gotcha. So, look, I'm willing to do this, but how do I know you're telling me the truth? It's a bit out there, and for all I know there's some human out there with advanced technology talking to me. And these people are innocent. How am I supposed to just take your word that they're some sort of…intergalactic criminals?"

"You don't have to believe me. You only need to do your job. And you have no choice."

"That's…okay. My *job* usually doesn't involve assassinating people, though. I don't know about where you come from, but this is a big deal for a human."

"That's enough questions. They're accomplishing nothing. If you continue to pester us, we'll cause you more pain."

"You gonna stab me in the brain again while I'm driving the car?" I chuckled. "Not your brightest idea."

"You'll park eventually and we'll deliver all the punishment at once. How does that sound?"

I grimaced. "All right. Fine. Your mission, your rules."

I fell silent, hoping Krause was listening. Hoping he wouldn't blow what had abruptly become something of an undercover operation. Hoping he'd keep his distance. Just…hoping.

Eventually the minutes of my ETA ticked down and we had made the shift from the city buildings into the closest thing to suburbia you got in these parts. The GPS guided me to a house on the right and I parked. Keeping my gaze on the house, I reached over blindly with my right hand and found my phone, sliding it into my jacket pocket as I stood up. Careful to avoid looking behind me as I exited the car, in case Krause had been following close, I stared at the home, knowing buying myself a minute or so could be helpful.

"Okay. So, what do you want me to do?"

"You are to enter the residence and kill all inside."

"All?" I asked, narrowing my eyes. "How many?"

"There should be three. An adult male and female and an adolescent male."

My stomach turned over and bile rose in the back of my throat. I suddenly pictured some helpless, clueless civilian being mentally tortured into coming to this house with a weapon and taking out a whole family. Could they even do it? Could some random person, from persistent torture, really murder two parents and a teenage boy? I gritted my teeth, my mind shifting to the image of them just slitting their own throat on the steps of this home rather than carry out a triple homicide from voices in their head.

"All right," I muttered. "Anything else I should know?"

"No."

Grimacing, I walked up the sidewalk to the front stoop and took the steps slowly. Taking a deep breath, I pressed the doorbell and then knocked loudly on the door. "NYPD. Responding to a noise complaint!" I shouted. "Anyone home?"

Pausing for a long moment to listen, I eventually heard footsteps and the door opened to a middle-aged man with a receding hairline, as average a person as I'd ever seen. "Hi, uh, sorry, you said a noise complaint?" he asked, looking baffled.

"Yes. Are you the only one home?"

"My wife and son are inside," he said, motioning with his hand. "But we're just having dinner."

"Can I come in?"

"Sure."

He stepped back and I took the handle of the door, pushing it a few inches short of shut behind me, and drew my gun from my holster. "Please show me where your family is."

The man froze, his eyes going from me to my gun and back again. "What is this?" he whispered. "Who are you?"

"Your family. Now."

"If you're here for-"

"Now," I said, raising the gun to his forehead.

He let out a whimper that hit me hard in the chest and stumbled back a few steps. "Okay, okay," he whispered. I lowered my gun to my side and motioned with my head. His eyes staying on me and my gun most of the way, he led me down the hall to the kitchen. "Elise, Camden," he said, his voice shaky as we entered the kitchen. "Can you- Can you get up from the table please?"

It seemed I'd interrupted them mid-dinner and there were expressions of confusion and then fear on their faces as the two of them did as the man had said. "Eric," Elise said, looking back and forth from me to him. "What's going on?"

"I'm here to kill you," I said, my face empty of emotion. "And I don't know why."

"No, no, no," the woman whimpered, shoving her son behind her as her husband rushed to her side. "Please, don't-"

"The voices in my head say you're not from Earth. Is that true?" I asked.

"What are you doing?" the female voice asked. The lack of emotion in her voice was jarring, as I'm sure she was irritated at the diversion from what she'd expected to be happening. "Kill them, now."

"We haven't hurt anyone on your planet," Eric cried, grasping his wife's arm tightly. "We're just hiding, and we've been here for years with no trouble. Please, we'll leave, we'll go somewhere else. Just don't hurt my family, *please*."

"I'm not going to," I told him, holstering my gun. "I could never do that. Do you have someone you can call to help you and the others on my planet? Your cover's been blown."

"What?" Eric asked, staring at me skeptically.

"What are you talking about?" the female voice asked in my head. "Do it, now."

"No."

A sword sliced its way through my skull and my vision went white as my knees gave out and I collapsed, screaming, clutching my head. The pain stopped and I blinked away spots in my vision, then it hit me again, and again, leaving me curled up and twitching on the floor.

"What's happening?" Eric asked. His voice was blurry, as was his face when I wearily looked up at him and saw he was knelt down next to me, remnants of the pain leaving my head ringing like a bell. "What are they doing to you?"

"Hell if I know," I breathed. "I'm just some puny Earthling. Are you hiding here because you hurt people?"

"No," Eric said, shaking his head furiously. "We're not criminals, we just-"

His voice cut out amidst another explosion of pain inside my skull. "Kill the family, now, or we will find someone who will," the female voice said in that absurdly calm, mechanical tone.

"No, you won't," I growled, clenching my fists in front of my forehead. "Because this is our planet, this is my country, and we don't execute innocent people here."

"They are not people."

"Looks like it's a transferrable rule of ethics for aliens, then," I snapped at the ridiculous counter argument.

"Stevens!" came a shout from outside. I heard the front door open and rapid footsteps down the hall until Krause came to an abrupt halt in the kitchen, his gun in his hand. "You okay?"

"Not really," I replied, staring up at him through half-lidded eyes.

"If you are not willing to carry this out, you are of no use to us," the male voice spoke.

"Then kill me," I said tiredly. "Or get out of my head. Because you just made too much noise and you've got no idea what humanity is capable of when we-"

My vision went white again as pain shot through my skull. I screamed, curling in on myself, screamed until my throat was raw and squeezed my eyes shut against the pain until tears leaked out the sides. Then the pain reached a place that pulled me down away from the world and darkness overtook me.

It only felt like a moment before I reopened my eyes, but clearly some time had passed, because I was laying on a couch. The family of three stood together on the side of the room, talking to my partner and a woman I didn't recognize. "What happened?" I asked blearily.

"Stevens," Krause snapped, rushing to my side. "How you feel? Your head okay?"

"I'm about a thousand miles of bad road, but I'll live, which is more than I thought when I passed out," I said, pushing myself to a sitting position. "Who's this?"

"You can call me Marilyn," the woman said. She looked about sixty, her gray hair hanging around her shoulders, and had the kind of expression on her face that let me think she wasn't one to often smile. "I'm in charge of…relocation."

Glancing up to Krause, I met his gaze. "You bring in anyone else on this?"

"I didn't even know if you were just losing your mind," he told me. "No, I didn't bring in anyone else. I've been off grid since I started following you."

Nodding, I pushed myself to my feet unsteadily. "Tell me I did the right thing," I said quietly to Marilyn. "Tell me I'm not helping you harbor war criminals or some crap like that."

"You're not," Krause told me, drawing my gaze. "They're just…refugees. It's a long story that apparently we're not privy to, but I got the gist of it. You did the right thing. Not that I could ever imagine you showing up at a random house and gunning down a family, no matter what you thought was going on."

I grunted softly. "What now?" I asked, directing my question toward Marilyn.

"This is, unfortunately, a war that's been going on for some time," she explained. "And Earth has nothing to do with it. We'll be relocating the surviving citizens."

"That's not good enough, because there's a woman out there who's going to have to plead insanity to a murder charge," I told her, jabbing my finger in the vague direction of the front door. "What gave you the right to put Earth's citizens in danger like that?"

Marilyn's lips parted in surprise, and she let out a breath. "That is…fair," she said, reluctantly. "I sincerely don't know how to resolve that."

Letting out a long breath and shaking my head, I glared at her. "There is no solving it. Unless you explain to the authorities what happened, and explain what you are. Because it's not just her; I know there were other victims too. The voices said they were making their way through a list."

The woman grimaced like she was sucking on a lemon and nodded. "They were."

"So. What do you suppose is the best way to do that?"
She blinked. "Do what?"

"Explain to the authorities, the people way over my head, what you are and why you're here?"

"We can't do that!" Marilyn exclaimed. "This is a legal issue from our end, and it's bad enough that word got out to you and your partner-"

"I don't care," I said softly, stepping closer to her. "You are on *our* planet. You're going to obey our rules. Those rules include not sending innocent people to prison. I'm not saying we should broadcast it over every news channel. I'm saying you are going to figure out how to fix what you did. To keep the woman I met this morning and the other victims out of prison. Teleport into the Oval Office and have a personal conversation with our president if you want, I don't care. I'm sure the ego of America will make sure the secret stays within a small circle. But someone with power needs to look out for the humans that were hurt because you used our planet as a safe house. And to make sure this doesn't happen again."

"She's right," Krause said, folding his arms. "So, your move. She just risked her life saving three of your citizens. How do we fix this for *our* citizens?"

Marilyn glanced at the family and then nodded slowly, looking back to me and my partner. "You're right. I can't argue with you on that. I'll talk to my superiors and, one way or another, we'll fix this."

I nodded once, looking over to the family, still huddled close together, as if they could be torn apart at any moment. This was the end of the line for me on this, I guessed, but whatever they were embroiled in was probably going to continue for the rest of their lives. A war, Marilyn had said. With innocents stuck in the middle. That was one thing I could understand as a human, at least.

And I wondered what would happen next. What would happen over the next few decades on Earth. Because of course, our government wouldn't be satisfied with just a chat. I had a feeling that this was going to be the start of something big. We'd looked up at the stars and wondered for millennia who and what was out there. Now we had our answer, and I knew it was just the beginning.